A Kentucky Dream

Susie Tillman

BEARHEAD PUBLISHING

- BhP -

Brandenburg, Kentucky

To: Mikayla

It is with great joy, I present

A Kentucky Dream

Susan Tillman

2017

BEARHEAD PUBLISHING

- BhP -

Brandenburg, Kentucky
.www.bearheadpublishing.com
A Kentucky Dream
by Susie Tillman

Cover Design by Bearhead Publishing
First Printing - October 2008
ISBN: 978-0-9799153-6-9
1 2 3 4 5 6 7 8 9 10

Disclaimer
This book is a work of fiction. The characters, names, places, and incidents are used fictitiously and are a product of the author's imagination. Any resemblance of actual persons, living or dead is entirely coincidental.

Proudly Printed in the United States of America.

Dedication

I dedicate this novel to God, for it is He who compelled me to write. I also dedicate this novel to Jack, my husband, family, and friends who encouraged me to step out of my comfort zone for this project. This is my labor of love for you all.

Acknowledgements

It is with the greatest gratitude I have for Bruce and Liz Henry, Mary Drechsel, and Audrey Cahill for their time, effort and suggestions for this project.

Chapter 1

While she scurried to make hot oatmeal and toast for the kiddos in her heavy, tan sweater and fuzzy, tan slippers, Nellie Bader added more wood to the black, cast iron, pot belly stove that sat next to the back door in the kitchen. Her husband, Alvin, had already eaten and had gone out to the barn to start the farm chores.

The eat-in kitchen was the second door on the left of the front foyer. It was a large room with two big, long windows with glass so old that it contained tiny bubbles. On this cold day, all the windows had a little frost in the corners.

On early winter mornings, this room had a chill until the stove got hot, but it didn't take long for 'Old Blacky' to do its job. Fresh-brewed coffee always helped to warm Nellie up as well. Her favorite flavor was hazelnut.

The big, old house was cold because it had no insulation. The small cellar, which was accessed from outside, contained the old boiler that wasn't large enough to really keep all the rooms warm. So the stove and fireplaces were used in the winter. The Baders hoped to someday update the heating and air.

Alvin's Christmas gift to Nellie, year before last, was having the neighbors help him update the kitchen. This wasn't a surprise gift since he wanted Nellie to pick out everything, within budget of course. Alvin had scrimped and saved sev-

1

eral years for this one, and his bride was so excited when he told her. Alvin felt that his sacrifice was more than worth it for his Nellie.

The appliances, cabinets, counter tops and linoleum were not the most expensive money could buy, but new. All these things gave the old kitchen a fresh look and a more efficient place for Nellie to do all her great cooking. Nellie practically lived in the kitchen when she wasn't quilting. There was always a bake sale or church bazaar to prepare for. Alvin preferred her homemade bread over store bought and always looked forward to every meal. Even the neighbors occasionally requested Nellie's bread. The recipe was given to her by her mother, Emma.

The old farm had been passed down from Alvin's parents, Ernest and Bertha Bader. Alvin and Nellie were a great team and didn't mind the chores and upkeep of the tree farm Ernest had begun. Besides, country living was much slower and not so high-tech as living in Louisville or bigger cities. It gave them a wonderful sense of belonging and a great place to raise their family.

The Baders sold wood to the furniture shop in town. They also prided themselves in having the prettiest Christmas trees in the state of Kentucky. The holiday trees were sold to the small hardware store on the corner in town or to folks who wanted to come and cut their own. Sometimes schools or churches in nearby towns would plan a hay ride into the forest to cut their Yule trees. Although many trees were planted for every one cut, the harvest wasn't always the best, but it was a living. Alvin used a special fertilizer with a secret formula that helped all the trees grow fast and healthy. The evergreens needed a more acidic fertilizer than other trees. Nevertheless, Alvin wasn't going to divulge his recipe to anyone. Only Nellie knew the ingredients in his concoction.

When Nellie quilted, she used Bertha's old quilting frame. Because quilting was a very time-consuming endeavor, Nellie produced only one or two a year. When Nellie and

Alvin were first married, she would often visit with Bertha and watch her quilt. It fascinated her how meticulous Bertha was with her stitching. Bertha had noticed Nellie's keen interest and carefully taught her daughter-in-law.

Alvin and Nellie first met in 1984 while attending a two-year community college in Louisville. Nellie was nineteen and Alvin was twenty. Nellie was slender and 5'4" with fair skin and thick, medium-brown hair that was short and curly. She rarely wore makeup, but really didn't need it. Her skin was as smooth as satin. Sentimental and melancholy would describe her best. Alvin thought Nellie was the greatest gal he had ever encountered. Alvin was first attracted to Nellie's beautiful skin and curls, but later he fell in love with her heart.

Alvin was tall and lanky with dark-brown hair, olive skin and a kind face. Nellie thought this gent was sweet and handsome. She knew almost instantly that he was the one. The couple had a lot in common. Both loved to dance and did so on many of their dates. After courting a couple of years, they married and settled in Shelbyville. Alvin's father passed away two years into their marriage, so they moved to the farm to help out Bertha. She died the next year when Nellie was expecting her first child, Sunnie. Since then, the Bader family has grown by three more children: David, Ethan and Jonas.

Nellie hollered up the steps to wake the children. "Sunnie, boys, it's time you all get up and help with the chores. It's goin' on seven o'clock. Daddy's already out in the barn." The children were allowed to sleep a bit later on the weekends; but on school days, wakeup came at six AM.

Every morning it was like pulling teeth to get the children out of bed. The colder the winter, the more they wanted to snuggle under the old quilts and comforters their grandmother, Bertha, had made. All the beds were soft and inviting and a great place to snuggle at the end of a busy day.

Sunnie was a pre-teen girl whose name described her disposition. She was also very, *very* nosey. At times, she

3

could ruffle everyone's feathers with obsessive talking. Being the oldest, Sunnie helped her parents with the care of her three brothers. Her dark-brown hair was shoulder length and curly. She inherited the curls from her momma. However, Sunnie definitely was Daddy's little girl and favored him in many ways. Sunnie had an olive complexion like Daddy which complimented her slender frame and pretty little face. She also always had a smile on her face and a golden tan in the summer which was so like her daddy.

Nellie and Alvin's only daughter had her own bedroom. The antique dresser was made of light wood and had a swivel mirror. The matching bed and nightstand were a little worn as was the lamp. Nellie's old dollhouse sat in one corner, and a toy chest sat at the foot of the bed. One year, Santa left chests for each child.

Upon hearing her momma's voice, Sunnie's eyes opened, and she quickly remembered the weatherman's report for snow. She ran to the window. Sure enough, there was a blanket of snow.....enough to make a snowman. It was unusual for it to snow so early in the winter. The biggest snows came mostly in February and March, but Sunnie always prayed for snow, especially on Christmas. She was smiling from ear to ear and quickly got dressed. Oh, how Sunnie loved the snow. It reminded her of all things fresh and pure, and Christmas, which was in just three weeks. She and her brothers liked to slide down the hill out back on an old inner-tube Daddy got for them.

Sunnie soon discovered that she was not the only one who had noticed the snow. She heard her brother, Jonas's high-pitched voice ring out, exclaiming, "It snowed!"

Ethan was eight and Jonas was six. Although they were not twins, the two boys looked very much alike and shared the same birthday. They were the best of friends. Nellie thought these guys were her special little men. Both were fair-skinned with dark-blonde hair and freckled noses. The boys were slender from playing and working hard. They very much enjoyed teasing Sunnie every chance they got.

Ethan and Jonas shared a bedroom. Their toy chests sat at the foot of their twin beds. A handmade bookcase sat on one side of the room and a double dresser on the other.

Ethan had now run over to take a look as well. As they glanced at each other, they shouted, "Snowman!!"

Ten-year-old David heard all the noise and asked, "What are you all shoutin' about?" Rubbing his eyes, he went to his window. "Snow, that's all Sunnie will be talkin' about," he mumbled quietly.

David also had his own room. He slept on the antique bed that had belonged to Granny Emma. There was a matching chest of drawers. His toy chest also sat at the foot of his bed. David was slender like Alvin with an olive complexion, light-brown hair, and a few freckles on his nose. He thought of himself as a big brother to his siblings, even Sunnie. Alvin thought of him as his top, right-hand man. After all, it was he who helped Daddy with most of the farm repairs.

David and his younger brothers shared a love for trains that began when their Uncle Bobby from Indiana built, in his yard, a miniature town with many model trains. While visiting their uncle, they loved to walk around this little town over and over again. Taking time out to eat was totally out of the question. All they wanted to do was explore every inch of this town. Uncle Bobby's unique creation started a hobby of collecting train memorabilia for his young nephews.

After dressing, the kids ran down the stairs to the kitchen where it was finally warm and toasty. There was a strong smell of fresh coffee brewing with a scent of toast and oatmeal in the background.

"Momma, it snowed!" Sunnie shouted as she got the orange juice out. "Can we go out and make a snowman?"

"No, the chores must be done first, and we need to go to the market," Nellie reminded Sunnie and all the kids.

"But Momma!" Sunnie whined with excitement over-coming her.

Nellie shook her head as she gave a glare, and Sunnie knew the subject was closed for now.

"Momma, do you think I can try some coffee today?" Sunnie asked, quickly changing the subject. "It always smells sooo good."

"You're still a little young for coffee, Sunnie. Maybe next year. You'll be thirteen then."

David just couldn't understand why Sunnie wanted to drink coffee so much. "That stuff tastes terrible. Why in the world do you want to drink it so bad?" he challenged, wrinkling his nose at his sister.

"Yeah, don't you know it stunts your growth?" Jonas and Ethan laughed.

"Listen boys, I like the smell. Besides I'm almost a teenager. That's close to bein' a grown-up," Sunnie argued, sitting up in her chair and throwing her head back like she was queen.

"You're not even close to bein' a grown-up!" David shouted.

"Children, stop your bickering and hurry on up with your breakfast!" Nellie ordered. There were chores to be done, and she needed to keep the children prepared for the day's tasks.

Ever obedient, the children all sat quietly and began shoveling food into their mouths. Sunnie, especially, wanted to finish eating as soon as possible. She knew the sooner she could get her chores done, the sooner she would be allowed to play in the snow.

When the children finished their breakfast, Nellie immediately began cleaning off the table while instructing her children, "Put on your boots, and go help Daddy." Nellie took the dishes over to the sink and began washing them while the children went out with Alvin.

The Baders liked raising their veggies and the critters they ate. The kids liked to name the animals, which made it hard come slaughter time; but they always gave the new animals the same names as the old. It just made it seem like they had never left. The siblings all got teary-eyed when it was time for each critter to go. Alvin had tried to teach them that that was just a part of farming.

Jonas was in charge of feeding the chickens and collecting the eggs. There was Millie, Annie, Betsy and Tom the rooster. Ethan fed the two hogs, Gertrude and Hilda. David helped Daddy clean out the barn and spread the fresh hay and was expected to help with repairs. Sunnie enjoyed her chore of feeding their two cows, Clara and Jenny. She talked to them as though they were people. She milked one and Daddy milked the other. George, the big tom-cat, lived in the barn, but he wasn't easy to catch or much of a pet. He ate a little cat food and the field mice that tried to make that old barn their home. Daddy only let him stay because he kept the number of mice down.

As far as Sunnie was concerned, they were missing the most important animals: a horse and goat. It was always her dream to be able to ride every day and have pets all her own, but Alvin didn't see a need to feed an animal they couldn't eat. They had an old tractor they used to plow the garden, so a horse was out of the question. They had cows for milk. Therefore, a goat wasn't needed either. On a farm, an animal that doesn't work or provide food is pure luxury, especially when money was tight. Sometimes Sunnie would run her mouth too much about "horse this" and "horse that", and Daddy's temper would finally flare. He would turn to Sunnie and look her right in the eyes. With a red face, Alvin would raise his voice to her, "Hush up about these useless animals, Sunnie!" Daddy's little girl knew not to say another word.

After the morning chores were done, the kiddos' noses were red. They were also starting to get a tingling in their toes, so back to the house they all went. Alvin headed out to the trees to make sure the snow hadn't done any damage to his precious crop.

"Children, go by the stove and warm up," Nellie told them. "After I put up the laundry, we girls are going into town to do our marketing," she said, giving Sunnie a smile.

Instead of returning Nellie's smile, Sunnie had a look of disappointment. She liked going into town and shopping with her momma. She was a bit let down to hear Momma's plan, because she was raring to go out and play in the snow. Her fun would just have to wait a little longer.

Looking toward the boys, Nellie told them, "Mr. Garrett just called and needs Daddy and you boys to help repair his fence before his cows get out. I think Jack is helpin' too."

Jack Garrett and David were the same age. They not only were schoolmates, but best friends; although David loved trains, Jack shared Sunnie's love for horses. Some of his other friends had horses, but that wasn't an animal they raised on his farm either. Like Sunnie, Jack wanted something he couldn't have.

Daddy was freezing when he came in the kitchen back door. Walking over to stand by the wood stove, he rubbed his hands together and told Nellie, "Well, the trees are all okay. The snow didn't really pull down the branches. It's really best if I just leave them be."

Nellie walked to the back hall door with Alvin and Sunnie following. As Nellie reached above a bench on the right hall wall and pulled down her coat from one of the hooks above, Alvin grabbed Nellie's shoulders and gave her a peck on the cheek. The children knew Daddy loved Momma because he was always winking at her or giving her a kiss. He sometimes lovingly referred to her as his bride. These small gestures always gave Sunnie and her brothers a secure and happy feeling.

Nellie told Alvin about the Garrett's fence and gave all her men goodbye smooches. After warming up, Alvin and the boys got into Daddy's tattered, light-blue Suburban and headed north to the Garrett farm, the next one up the road.

Nellie and Sunnie stepped out the back door and onto a small wood deck that the Bader boys helped their daddy build. The projects seemed to be never-ending.

The exterior of the farmhouse had old aluminum siding that had been painted taupe a few years ago. The house had a tin roof which needed painting. This was the next major project to save for. The family would need the help of neighbors as they did for the barn and garage. The Baders were good at returning favors and lending a helping hand to their fellow farmers, as they would be with the Garrett's fence today.

To the left of the house, was a gravel driveway leading up to the one-car, wood-framed garage which had an attached carport on the right. The garage and carport had fresh taupe paint and the barn fresh red paint. The gravel butted against the concrete stoop just outside the kitchen door and went a little farther toward the barn. To the right of the stoop were the wooden doors to the cellar. Alvin installed a new water heater down there last year.

The girls backed out of the small garage in the red Chevy truck which was old and weathered. They slowly drove to town as the roads were a little slushy.

Sunnie asked, "When we get home, can I call Kim and Kelly to come down and help build a snowman?" Kim and Kelly were the Garrett's twin girls. They were also Sunnie's best friends. They all went to school together and played often. Jack was their not-so-much younger brother. Their mom, Barbara Garrett, and Nellie were friends as well. These women shared recipes, crafts, worked at the church bazaars and spent Derby days together.

"We'll call after lunch and see if it's okay with Barbara."

The scenery on the way to town was beautiful. As the old truck passed the adjacent farm, the rolling fields on the old

Hayfield place glistened with the fresh fallen, untouched snow. It looked like tightly packed cotton. What a sight for Sunnie's eyes.

"Momma, it's a shame Mr. Hayfield died. His farm is so beautiful. What will happen to it?"

"Well, I hear it's up for sale. I don't think his daughter, Shelby, wants it since she lives in Chicago."

"Maybe Daddy can buy it. He would have more fields for his trees," Sunnie suggested, her eyes glowing with enthusiasm.

"Oh, Sunnie girl, that farm was in Hayfield's family for generations. There's more acreage there than the law allows. It must be worth at least a half-million dollars. We don't have that kind of money." Nellie was trying to be attentive with her driving while answering Sunnie's many questions.

"A half-million dollars! Really?" Sunnie asked. Her enthusiasm faded as quickly as it had arisen. With a sad expression, Sunnie looked back at the Hayfield farm.

"At least, maybe more," Nellie assured her.

"I wonder who will buy it," Sunnie pondered aloud in a much quieter voice.

"Only time will tell, Sunnie. Only time will tell," Nellie added.

As they passed the beautiful acreage, Sunnie kept staring out the truck window and silently daydreaming about the farm's future. Who would be their next neighbors?

Chapter 2

Pleasureville was a small town six miles down the road with a population of 870. It was primarily residential with a few businesses and two churches. The town had one small grocery with a little café to the left of the two checkout counters. This market was located between the furniture store and the apothecary, which had a post office in it. The only mercantile store was small and sat across the street. The hardware store was next to it followed by the feed/hay market. The town wasn't big enough for a hospital, only a clinic with a visiting doctor and nurse. Down a side street was a very small police station with only two officers, John and Adam. The station was located next to the clinic and across from the small, county elementary and high schools. As in most small towns, everyone knew everyone and helped one another.

Sunnie always liked to window shop and people watch. When the weather permitted, she would sit on the bench in front of the grocery store and watch people come and go. She loved to chat with everyone.

"It's much too cold for you to be sittin' on the bench today, Sunnie. You need to come inside with me. You can wait in the front of the store if you like," Nellie told her.

So while her momma shopped, Sunnie stood in the front and watched out the window of the grocery store. After a few minutes, a very fancy car pulled up and parked next door in front of the furniture store. Sunnie stared and took in all the details as she always loved to do. The car must have been very expensive. It was beige with a large hood ornament and a fancy, black sign on the door that said *'Willow Farm'*.

Mr. Perkins was standing behind Sunnie unbeknownst to her. "If that don't beat all! That looks like a Rolls Royce!" he commented, causing Sunnie to nearly jump out of her skin.

Half scared out of her wits, she turned and looked up at the store's owner. Mr. Perkins was medium in height with a little belly in spite of his skinny frame. His hair was grey and balding on top. He also sported a bushy grey mustache. Mr. Perkins always wore suspenders and a white apron around his waist and smelled of Old Spice cologne.

"I didn't know you were there, Mr. Perkins. You scared me half to death," Sunnie told him, still holding her hand to her heart. "What's a Rolls Royce anyway?" she asked after calming down a bit.

"Only one of the most expensive cars money can buy, my dear girl. Wonder who could be in that?" he said as he squinted staring out the window at the car. He was so engrossed in trying to figure out who this rich person could be that he never even apologized to Sunnie for having frightened her. "Sunnie, you watch and tell me what's goin' on. I have too much stock to put out to just stand here," he finally concluded. Mr. Perkins knew he was safe to walk away. Sunnie would give him the scoop and not leave out a single detail.

"I sure will, Mr. Perkins!" Sunnie readily agreed, her nosy demeanor kicking in full gear. As Mr. Perkins went on about his work, Sunnie went outside to take in everything. The driver got out, came around and opened the back door. He was dressed in a black suit. Sunnie briskly walked up to the car. Her eyes widened as she watched the passenger from the back seat step out of the car with the help of the driver. Perhaps in her early sixties, the woman was a tall, sophisticated lady. Her hair was straight, salt and pepper in color, and styled in a short bob. She was dressed in a brown fur coat, brown leather gloves, and boots. A small part of her beautiful, rust-colored sweater was showing around her neck.

Sunnie looked up at the lady, her eyes widening further and her mouth dropping open. The elegant lady glanced down at Sunnie as she stepped onto the walkway and said with a friendly smile, "Good morning young lady. I imagine you are excited about all this snow."

Flabbergasted, Sunnie said quietly, "Good mornin'. Yes, I love the snow."

Sunnie thought to herself that there weren't many rich people around these parts. The lady went into the furniture store. Although it was a small town, this store was well known for its beautiful, handmade-to-order furniture. Sunnie looked at the car again and noticed the driver waiting at the car's back door. The driver saw her staring and gave her a gentle nod. She was surprised at his gesture and was a little embarrassed. Then she quickly stepped up to watch through the store window hoping not to be noticed. The lady was apparently putting in a furniture order. Sunnie was used to watching customers go in to order. It seemed like an eternity when the lady finally turned and headed out of the store. Sunnie backed away from the window and waited for her. As the woman stepped onto the walkway, she slipped and her handbag went flying down the walk with several items spilling out. The driver quickly stepped up to help steady her on her feet.

"Are you okay, ma'am?" Sunnie shouted. "Let me pick up your purse and stuff."

"I am fine. Thank you for assisting me. I really appreciate your help," she replied, sounding a bit shaken.

Sunnie handed the lady her handbag after placing the items back in it. Standing and staring with amazement, Sunnie smiled at the lady.

"It was nice of you to gather my handbag. Do you live around here?" asked the lady.

"Yep, we have a farm on Highway 561. Do you live around here?" Sunnie didn't hesitate to ask.

"No, I live in Lexington, but maybe we will be neighbors some day," she said surprising Sunnie, who was pleased when she then asked, "Young lady, what is your name?"

"It's Sunnie," she chirped with a wide smile.

"What a pretty name," the stranger commented, gently touching Sunnie's cold nose. Smiling, she added, "I am Mrs. Willow. Perhaps I will see you again when I am in town. Now I must go. It is cold, and I have to attend to some business. Goodbye for now," she said quietly.

"I hope I will see you again too," Sunnie told her as she watched the woman walk over to the expensive car. "Goodbye," Sunnie said while waving as the driver helped Mrs. Willow back into the car. The man in black tipped his hat to Sunnie, making her day. Then he got back into the large car and drove off.

With a red nose, Sunnie went bouncing back into the grocery store. Nellie was at the check-out. "Sunnie, I thought I told you to stay inside!" she scolded with a hint of anger in her eyes.

Sunnie's face was beaming. "Momma, wait 'till I tell you what just happened. I need to tell Mr. Perkins too."

"He's busy right now. You can talk to him on our next visit. Help me out with the groceries. We need to stop at the hardware store and get a few things for Daddy. Then you can tell me all about it on our drive home," Nellie rushed on, totally preoccupied with the business at hand. Besides, Sunnie was always going on about something.

"But Momma, something excitin' just happened!" Sunnie persisted.

Nellie reinforced, "Never mind. Let's get done with our errands, and I'll listen on the way home."

"But this is important stuff!" Sunnie insisted, feeling as if she were about to burst wide open at the seams.

Nellie shook her head and gave that glare again. Although it was hard for her not to run her mouth, Sunnie knew enough not to press her luck at this point. She knew

Momma had an agenda and would give her undivided attention later.

So Sunnie went quietly, helped her mother with the groceries, and after stowing them in the back of the truck, walked obediently at her mother's side to the hardware store. The hardware store, although small, seemed to have one of everything. The girls looked for the owner, Mr. Taylor. He was on the tall, but plump, side. This man carried a pipe full of cherry tobacco in his mouth and always had dirty hands from moving the stock around. He was very helpful to all his customers' needs. Daddy knew him well since he seemed to know how to fix almost anything.

"Hi there, ladies," Mr. Taylor exclaimed, his pipe waving at them as his lips moved. "Alvin called yesterday and told me what he needed. It's here in the box," he said, placing his hands on a nearby cardboard container. Glancing at Sunnie, he frowned, saying, "Sunnie, you look frozen. Go over by the stove while your momma settles up." As he watched the girl head toward the stove, he turned his attention back to Nellie and began making small talk, "Well, we got our first snow. I know my boy, Patrick, sure is happy. He would rather be home playin' in it instead of helpin' me out today, but I had extra stock to put away. Patrick loves for it to snow on Christmas."

"Sunnie loves the snow too, even more so than the boys. I guess it's because Alvin always has them help shovel around the house and barn," said Nellie.

"It will be twenty dollars, Nellie. Tell the boys I said hi," Mr. Taylor replied.

"I'll be sure to tell them," Nellie said as she handed Mr. Taylor a twenty dollar bill. Gathering her purse, she turned and called to her daughter, "Come on Sunnie; let's go so you can play in the snow after lunch."

As they were driving home, Sunnie couldn't wait any longer to tell Momma who she met. "Guess who I talked to while you were shoppin'?"

"Well, you're pretty excited. It must be someone important."

"I met a new friend today!" Sunnie said excitedly.

"Who might that be?" Nellie asked, taking her eyes briefly off the road to glance at her daughter.

"A *grand* lady named Mrs. Willow," Sunnie gushed, her eyes twinkling with delight.

"That name doesn't sound familiar. I don't believe I know this Mrs. Willow," Nellie replied with narrowed eyes.

"She said she lives in Lexington. She was in this *huge*, expensive car with a driver. Mr. Perkins said it was a Rolls Royce, whatever that is. She had on a fur coat. When her fancy car pulled up, I just had to go outside and see what was goin' on. The car had *'Willow Farm'* on the side."

"What did she say to you, Sunnie?" Nellie asked. She was a little curious about this lady, but she also wanted to be sure that Sunnie had minded her manners and not been too forward with this visitor to their little town.

"She wanted to know my name, and she thought my name was pretty. She went to order furniture, I guess. Mrs. Willow said we might be neighbors some day. She must be a very busy lady because she had a lot of business to attend to. Wonder what kind of business that is?"

"Well it's hard to say. There are a lot of well-to-do people in Lexington. Perhaps she has somethin' to do with horses. Lexington is full of horse farms," Nellie commented, figuring this lady was just someone passing through. She was surprised someone of her social status had taken the time to talk to her daughter.

"Oh, do you think so? I wish I could visit her and see these horses!"

"Well I'm only guessin'. We really don't know what she does there, but I can't imagine why she would be our neighbor unless, ...ummm."

"Unless what Momma?"

16

"Never mind. I would only be guessin', and I don't like spreadin' rumors. We need to get on home," Nellie said, bringing an end to the conversation about the wealthy stranger.

"I can't wait to tell Kim and Kelly about my new friend when they come over!" Sunnie said as she added one last comment.

Pulling into the driveway, Nellie said, "You can call Kim and Kelly while I get lunch ready." Nellie could see so much excitement in Sunnie's face. She grinned to herself and knew Sunnie would dream and talk about this lady for days to come. Sunnie had never met anyone that was rich before.

Daddy and the boys came in just as Nellie finished heating some chili and fixing grilled cheese sandwiches for lunch. "Mm, somethin' smells mighty good," Alvin sniffed.

While they were eating, Sunnie told the guys all the details of her encounter with this mystery woman. The boys took the story in with a grain of salt. It was just another excuse for their sister to run her mouth. At one point, David blurted, "Blah, blah, blah and blah, blah." Sunnie gave her brother a hard, cold stare, but that didn't stop her from telling the *whole* story. Alvin was also curious as to what this woman was doing here and why she might be a neighbor someday; but he figured Sunnie would be the first to have *the entire* scoop, so he put his thoughts to other matters.

After lunch, Kim and Kelly Garrett came over with their brother Jack to help build a snowman. Sunnie gathered up the items for the project. To the right of the oak front door was a recently added, large closet that jutted out into the foyer. In this closet, the Baders had a special box with 'Snowman' written on it. It contained a scarf, hat, several lumps of coal, and a hand-carved carrot made of wood that Sunnie had painted. David and Jack were in charge of making the first big ball. Sunnie, Kim and Kelly had to roll the next one. Jonas and Ethan rolled the head. Of course during all this activity, Sunnie was jabbering about Mrs. Willow, her new acquaintance. After awhile, her brothers told her to shut up. They had heard all they wanted to hear, but the twins were entertained by it and wanted to hear more.

A couple of hours later, Nellie made all the children come in to dry their clothes and warm up. They had hot chocolate and freshly baked chocolate chip cookies while they played a card game, Go Fish, at the kitchen table. Sunnie only gave half her attention to the game. She was still thinking of the lady from Lexington. Would she ever see her again?

Chapter 3

At supper, David asked if they could go into the field the next day and cut a Christmas tree. Sunnie usually was the first to ask, but she was consumed with this Mrs. Willow thing.

"We'll go first thing after we get back from church tomorrow. I'll put the tree in the stand and start putting on the lights while Momma fixes lunch. You kids are in charge of the ornaments, as usual. Nellie, don't forget to bake some of your delicious cookies to leave out for Santy Claus," Alvin exclaimed. Alvin was a big kid at Christmas and a great believer in ol' St. Nick. He loved all their family traditions, from selecting the tree, putting out the cookies, and waking up at the crack of dawn on Christmas morning to see what Santa had brought. Watching his family open gifts made him feel like Santa himself. Alvin was truly the biggest kid of all.

Nellie always got the children involved in gift shopping and wrapping. All the kids really enjoyed giving presents, especially the ones they made. For Nellie, it was a very senti-mental time of the year. She would occasionally get teary-eyed because she missed her parents who had passed away. Christmas time brought back memories of her happy childhood and all the special things they did as a family. 'Silent Night' was the carol that made her cry. During this holy time, Nellie would always count her blessings and give special thanks. She had her man, who was the love of her life, the greatest kids in the world, and the old farm, which she loved.

The Baders always attended church on Sundays. They went to a small, Christian church near town that looked like a little white church in Vermont. The family always sat near the front on the left. Alvin and Nellie impressed upon the children that everything was possible with Jesus. It was important to keep Him in your heart.

The preacher, Pastor Noah, was in his mid-forties. He was tall and lean with a kind, but handsome face. He had steel blue eyes and dark blonde hair. When he smiled, his teeth looked like pearls. The pastor had a habit of tilting his head to his left as he preached, and he had a special gift of applying the gospel to today's life. He also managed to get the congregation to laugh, which made it fun to learn what he was teaching. Nellie liked to listen to Pastor Noah's message, but she enjoyed the church music most of all. Music was her connection to the Holy Spirit.

The organist, Anna Rose, had the most beautiful, thick, grey hair and pretty green eyes. This made her the envy of many of the lady parishioners. She always dressed to the tee, and all her accessories coordinated with her attire. Anna Rose was a talented musician and a teacher at the elementary school.

At the farm after church, everyone changed into work clothes. Alvin hooked up the wagon to the old tractor, which had seen better days. A few years back, after a family effort of scrubbing and waxing, Daddy had taken ol' faithful to display at the Kentucky State Fair. Now all bundled up, the Baders went out to the fields to pick out that perfect Christmas tree. Alvin made sure there were several to choose from.

Alvin knew which tree was to be their Christmas tree just as soon as he laid eyes upon it…a six-foot, full-branched, blue spruce; the family's usual pick. David walked beside Daddy, holding the chain saw. Then Alvin reached to take the saw from his oldest son.

Nellie, Sunnie, Ethan and Jonas stood, watched and listened to the 'ziz ziz ziz' as Alvin sawed the trunk almost in two. "Bout ready for some brawn," Alvin announced to all his children with an amused smile. Then he stepped away and stood with Nellie as they watched the kids push the tree down. It landed with a soft thud on the hard, frozen ground.

Alvin and his family dragged the tree a short distance to the tractor. Then, everyone helped to lift and secure it safely in the wagon. With proud expressions on all their faces, they piled along the sides of the tree. Even though it was a little hard finding room to ride back with that big tree, they managed to squeeze in.

Lunch went ever so quickly. Everyone couldn't wait to get to the job at hand. Because the tree was so fresh, it filled the living room with a seasonal aroma. Decorating it would be sooo much fun. Nellie always put on some old Christmas music. Everyone would sing along, but Daddy's singing was a little off key. Nellie was sure he was tone deaf, but she would harmonize as best she could. When Sunnie tried to follow, the boys would laugh and tell her that she would never be a singer. But surprisingly, they sang quite well considering their youthfulness. The little guys liked 'Jingle Bells' and 'Santa Claus is Coming to Town'. As usual, the waterworks came down Nellie's face when the Baders sang 'Silent Night'.

The kids carefully placed the ornaments as though to create a masterpiece. Alvin had a few tattered ornaments from his childhood. His favorite was the old fire truck with a wreath on the grill. Nellie had a few of her own, one of which was an old metal carrot with the paint peeling. The Baders also had a collection of ornaments that were purchased from every church bazaar. Each child had several ornaments they made at the craft workshops that Barbara Garrett held at the church. The children placed those in the same area of the tree each year. Having this routine held down the bickering.

Nellie laid some greenery on the mantel and added some special decorations around the room. The wreath Alvin made for the front door was large. He made it from the branches that were removed from the bottom of the tree. Boy, did all that greenery put out a wonderful, wintery scent. The red bow Daddy placed at the top of the wreath had seen its better days. Momma had made it about six years ago.

As Nellie glanced over her holiday décor making sure every piece was placed perfectly, she said, "By the way, don't forget Uncle Bobby, Aunt Debbie and your cousins Donna and Lonnie are comin' Christmas Eve and stayin' until afternoon Christmas day." Nellie saw her brother, Bobby, only a few times a year because he lived in Greenville, Indiana. "David, you and Lonnie can bunk up with Ethan and Jonas. Your aunt and uncle can sleep in your room. I'll get out the sleepin' bags. It will be like campin' out. Sunnie, you girls will have fun gigglin' and laughin'. Aunt Alice, Uncle Jerry, Steve and Tim will be here Christmas mornin' around eleven o'clock." Alice was one of Alvin's siblings, Cheryl was the other.

About every other year, Aunt Cheryl and Uncle Tom would also come with their kids: Cortnee, Samantha, and Benjamin. Sunnie was closer to her cousin, Cortnee, than all the rest. They had very similar personalities. At times, the girls would finish each other's sentences. At least once a month, Momma would let Sunnie call Cortnee, but their conversations had to stay short. Sunnie was always sad when they didn't come for Christmas. Alvin dearly loved his sisters and missed them when they weren't together for the holidays. Alice and Cheryl loved being at their childhood home on Christmas. The

Baders were big on family gatherings. The more the merrier is how they felt.

David shouted, "We'll have a blast won't we guys?"

"Yeah," the boys simultaneously stated. They loved it when they spent time with Uncle Bobby. He was always adding new things to his miniature town and trains. Bobby's son, Lonnie, was a train lover too. So the boys and Uncle Bobby could talk endlessly about trains. Although Alvin was fascinated with Bobby's many talents, he was a tree lover at heart.

"Just what I need, more train talk," Sunnie complained.

"Quit your whinin', Sunnie. You have your Mrs. Willow talk, they have their train talk. Besides, I can't wait to see them all. It's great when everyone comes for Christmas. Family is one of the most important things, missy. Try to remember that," Alvin stated, reminding Sunnie.

Nellie barked out, "Well there is much work to do before then. You kids need to help with my to-do list, and that includes helpin' to bake our special cookies. We have everyone's gifts, so we can wrap a few each night after supper until it's done."

"I'll help you, Momma," Sunnie promised.

The next week was busy and the snow, of course, melted. The snowman's outfit was tucked away and waiting for the next snow.

The girls had to make another trip into Mr. Perkins' grocery to pick up food for the Christmas holidays. Sunnie couldn't wait to tell him about her new friend. Nellie parked the truck and before she could shut off the engine and get out, Sunnie had run into the store shouting to Mr. Perkins who was standing near the checkout trying to assist a customer. Sunnie abruptly interrupted, "Mr. Perkins, guess who that was in that Rolls-whatever?"

"Sunnie, it's a Rolls Royce," he told her with an amused smile.

"Yeah, yeah, Rolls Royce!" Sunnie blurted out.

"Be patient. I'll be with you when I am finished with Mrs. Bartley. Now apologize to her for interrupting," Mr. Perkins said in a raised voice. Although he loved to gossip, his customers always came first.

"I'm sorry Mrs. Bartley. I'm just excited right now." The customer nodded as Mr. Perkins briefly left the area to get a product for her. The time he was gone seemed like an eternity to this impatient, nosy girl. She stood there tapping her foot with her arms folded.

When Mr. Perkins returned, he explained a few things to Mrs. Bartley and bid her farewell. This man adored Sunnie as if she was his own grandchild, but she did have a way of making a nuisance of herself. As Mr. Perkins placed his hands on Sunnie's shoulders, he said, "Now try to calm down as you give me the whole scoop. At this point, Mr. Perkins was ready for some real good gossip.

"It's a rich lady named Mrs. Willow. She lives in Lexington. She said she might be my neighbor someday, and she thinks I have a pretty name," Sunnie gloated as she rambled with constant hand gestures.

"You don't say," Mr. Perkins said with his hand upon his chin and a puzzled look on his face.

"There was a man all dressed up in black that drove her car and helped her in and out of it! She almost fell on the walk and dropped her purse. I picked it up, and she thanked me for helping her. Mr. Perkins, I've never had a rich friend before," Sunnie shared, her face absolutely glowing.

"Well, well." He paused for a second. "I don't recall anyone quite so wealthy ever bein' in our town. You said she might be your neighbor someday. I wonder what that's supposed to mean."

"I hope my new friend moves here."

After stopping and speaking to a neighbor in front of the store, Nellie came into the grocery. Walking up and catching the last of Sunnie's conversation, Nellie said, "You don't suppose this Mrs. Willow's buyin' the Hayfield farm do you, Mr. Perkins? We've heard that his daughter, Shelby, didn't want it since she lives in Chicago and all."

"You might just have somethin' there, Nellie. That's a point well taken," Mr. Perkins agreed, holding up his index finger. "But only time will tell."

"Oh, I hope you all are right. I would pass by Mrs. Willow's farm all the time!" Sunnie exclaimed.

"Well Sunnie, I can't stand here and chatter all day, there's too much to do back home," Nellie said with her hands on her hips and thoughts more on Christmas chores. "Come, let's get to the shoppin'."

"See you later, Mr. Perkins," Sunnie said, giving a little wave. Then both Nellie and Sunnie said almost together, "Merry Christmas and Happy New Year!"

The girls started down the grocery aisle. The food mart had a few scrawny decorations about, but they weren't anything to write home about. Since Mr. Perkins was a widower, he wasn't very interested in decorating.

Sunnie and Nellie's conversation with Mr. Perkins set off a buzz in Pleasureville throughout the holidays. Of course, everyone had Mrs. Willow moving to the Hayfield farm. What was it going to be like having someone so rich living nearby? Would she be happy living in a small community? The gossipers wondered if she had a husband. Surely he must be a strong, handsome man; a great entrepreneur of sorts.

Five days prior to Christmas Eve, Nellie and the kids baked cookies for hours. They gave tins of cookies to neighbors and the store owners in town. Of course, there were plenty left to enjoy throughout the Christmas holidays. The cookies for Santa were large Santa's and reindeer decorated with icing. There would be one from each of the Bader kids and two from their visiting cousins, six in all. They were put on a plate that had a Santa face in the center, then placed on the hearth. It was surprising that Alvin didn't have one on the plate especially from him.

Christmas Eve morning, Sunnie was excused from her barn chores to help Momma bake three pies. They made pumpkin, of course, and apple and pecan. Nellie whipped up fresh cream to top them. While baking, Nellie mixed up the cranberry relish everyone seemed to love. The turkey and dressing were also baked on Christmas Eve. After cooling, the turkey was sliced, put in a casserole dish, and then covered with gravy. That was everyone's favorite. All this early preparation allowed Nellie to enjoy her guests when they arrived.

When the men came into the house from doing the chores, they all inhaled deeply and smiled. Mm, mm! What an aroma. The delicious moment soon ended though, as Nellie began to divvy out important tasks to all of them. "Alvin, you're in charge of makin' the apple cider and lemonade. Remember we need enough for tonight and tomorrow. Boys, you carry in more firewood so we can keep the fires burnin'. Stack it neatly by the wood stove and both fireplaces. Sunnie, here's the fixins' for the dip and cheese ball. You've helped me enough in the past. I think you're ready to make them by yourself." Nellie was a little bossy. She had her way of doing everything efficiently, so she did the delegating. They all frowned but really didn't mind. Alvin and the kids just liked to give Nellie a hard way to go while they grinned to themselves. It was important to Nellie that she did a good job at pulling off all the festivities for her guests and family.

The day had passed quickly since there was much to do before company arrived. Supper was a quick bowl of homemade vegetable soup and crackers.

"Okay men, hurry upstairs and get cleaned up. Our family will be here very soon," Nellie demanded as she and Sunnie finished cleaning up the kitchen. Nellie always made sure the parlor had candles burning. It created a magnificent smell throughout the house and added a warm cozy feeling.

Occasionally she was called Martha Stewart II by her neighbors and friends, but she knew she couldn't hold a candle to that icon. Although it was fun trying, Nellie's homemaking style was geared more to the country way of life. After all, they bought very little of what was needed to live. Time seemed to stand still, and the kids were getting more excited by the minute waiting for their company to arrive.

Chapter 4

At seven o'clock, there was a 'knock, knock at the door. Nellie's brother and his family had arrived. Alvin exclaimed, "Welcome, welcome. It's so good to see you all. Give me your coats. Come in and warm up by the fire. We've got a lot to catch up on. Boys, please take their suitcases upstairs." After Alvin hung up the coats, he and Nellie hugged everyone.

"Is there anything I can help you do for tomorrow?" Debbie offered as she handed Nellie her homemade sweet rolls and carried a large pot of green beans to the kitchen.

"No thanks. Most of the hard stuff is done. We'll cook the sweet potatoes and bake the bread tomorrow after breakfast while the rest is warming up. Alice is bringin' her delicious dumplins'."

Debbie ooohed. "Ah, yes. I love those dumplings. I believe her mom passed down that recipe." Looking all about, she praised with an appreciative smile, "Nellie this kitchen still looks great. Alvin did a wonderful job with the remodeling."

"The best part about it is I have a place for everything now and more counter space," Nellie shared. Debbie was good at decorating and gardening. Nellie liked to get ideas from her, so she was pleased by Debbie's compliments about her kitchen. Lightly touching her sister-in-law's arm, Nellie suggested with eagerness, "Let's go into the parlor and catch up."

As Nellie walked a little behind Debbie, she quickly gave her an appraising glance. Debbie's petite figure made her appear to be much younger than she was. Deb dressed in a conservative manor with a splash of bright color here and there. She always wore the same cologne, Jessica McClintock. Nellie's nose picked up a whiff of the pleasant smell. Debbie had a real classy look about her. Nellie admired Debbie, but would never spend money on expensive things like her sister-in-law.

As the family gathered in the parlor, it became a festive place. The living room was across from the kitchen. It had one window facing the room's entrance and two at the front of the house. A stone fireplace was on the back, left wall with a crackling fire. A lovely, large, old oriental rug was in the center of the room with furniture surrounding the edges. To the left of the fireplace was a TV on a stand in the corner.

Alvin's hot apple cider seemed to hit the spot along with Sunnie's cheese ball and dip. Of course, she boasted how she made it all by herself this year. The first thing out of the boys' mouths was to ask Uncle Bobby about any new additions to his train village. He was constantly enlarging it.

"Well I have a surprise that will answer your questions," Bobby announced. He had brought a video showing his little town of Swiftcreek. Everyone was glued to the TV. You could hear the overlapping of everyone talking, "Would you look at that. How did you make that? That looks so real. When can we come and see it?" As time progressed, Bobby was sure he had chosen the right gift for the Bader boys and his son, Lonnie.

Uncle Bobby was short with extremely dark hair. His skin was dark from working outside with his landscaping business. Nellie's brother had many talents, which included drawing and rebuilding cars. She thought he was not only talented but quite adorable. Nellie was just a little bias.

The whole evening you could hear the hum of many conversations and laughter. Occasionally, the kids were told to calm down. Since the cousins didn't see each other often, they would often roughhouse while playing. They were also excited about Santa and opening gifts in the morning.

Alvin looked at his watch and saw it was already ten-thirty. "Okay, boys and girls. We need to leave ol' Santy his snack, then everyone needs to head up to bed. You know we always get up with the chickens to see what the jolly dude has left." Alvin made a mental note to set his alarm extra early so he could do his farm chores before everyone got up.

"Alvin, you're not getting us up at the crack of dawn like you did last Christmas are you?" Bobby asked, frowning. Alvin nodded with a smirk on his face. "I can see there's no negotiation on this one." Uncle Bobby should have known better. Getting up early on Christmas morning was a given. All in all, it was a fun tradition. Alvin made it that way.

"Nellie and I will tidy up and batten down the hatches. You all go on up and go fast asleep."

All the children helped put the cookies and milk near the fireplace and headed upstairs with anticipation. Alvin was the greatest believer in 'ol St. Nick. The older children followed his lead.

Sunnie prayed again for a Christmas snow as she snuggled in with Donna. Unlike the boys, they were in a hurry to get to sleep. Sunnie tried, but most Christmas Eves she didn't sleep well. She was much like her daddy in that way. The boys were having a wrestling match until Nellie told them to behave or Santa wouldn't come. They finally calmed down and dozed off.

Alvin and Nellie quietly scurried to place their family gifts under the tree. Bobby had given them the keys to the van so they could put their family gifts under the tree as well. If they didn't get to bed soon, Santa wouldn't come. It always was a tiring two days, but Alvin couldn't wait to wake everyone up early on Christmas morning.

Five AM. came way too soon, but Nellie got up with Alvin to help with the chores. They quickly started up the stove in the kitchen. As they stepped out the back, they saw the ground was dusted with snow. Sunnie's prayer had been answered. "Hurry up, Nellie. We need to wake everyone up soon," said Alvin.

"Hold your horses, Alvin. We'll be done in plenty of time. You're worse than the kids when it comes to Christmas and Santa."

"You know how much I've always loved this time of year. It's very special for me. I know it is for you too. Now let's get goin'."

The chores went a little faster than usual. They skipped the things that didn't need immediate attention. With Alvin holding onto Nellie's arm, he dragged her along at a quick pace back toward the house. She was grinning and thought to herself that he must be her biggest kid.

They took off their dirty boots on the back porch and washed up. Alvin looked at the kitchen clock. It was twenty till six, which was just enough time for Alvin to build a fire in both fireplaces. Nellie put on a pot of coffee and got out the dishes and sweet rolls. Debbie's rolls were a Christmas morning tradition. Alvin rushed upstairs and started banging on all the bedroom doors. "Wake up little chillens 'cause Santy Claus has come!!"

Sunnie looked out her bedroom window as she did every morning and saw the dusting of snow. This was going to be the best Christmas ever she thought. She quickly darted out of her room as did her cousins. It was a rule that everyone must wait in the hall so they could all go downstairs together.

With sleepy eyes, Uncle Bobby and Aunt Debbie came into the hall. "Oh Alvin, why so early?" Bobby complained, but Alvin just grinned.

David shouted, "Come on everybody. Let's go and see what Santy left." There was a mad dash with the kids nearly knocking down the grownups on the stairs.

Alvin always started Christmas day off with a prayer. "Okay folks. Before we open our gifts, let's give thanks." He folded his hands and bowed his head. "Lord, thank you for the best and most precious gift of all, your son, Jesus. We thank you for all our many blessings, and we pray for those in need. It's in your son's name we pray. Amen."

Sunnie was first to open her gifts. The tradition was to open gifts oldest to youngest child one year, then the opposite on the next. Sunnie was so excited as she looked at a large box that lay at her feet. As she quickly opened the gift, she soon saw that it was a large ceramic colt that was lying down. The style of painting made it almost look real.

Alvin snickered as he spoke, "Sunnie, it's okay for you to keep *this* horse. I'm sure we can find room in the barn. I don't imagine he'll eat much. What are you going to name him?"

"Oh Daddy, I'll find somethin' to feed him, and I need to think about his name," she said as she hugged Momma and Daddy giving kisses and thank-yous.

Donna received a beautiful new winter coat. It was classy and had Debbie's taste written all over it. Uncle Bobby made sure all the boys received an old-time locomotive. They were not quite as expensive as his models, but still of good quality. Their eyes and mouths were open so wide that flys could have found a home. The Baders had given Bobby a gift certificate to his favorite hobby shop. Debbie had been given one of Nellie's quilts. She sort of expected it since she had picked out the pattern, but seeing it was another story. Its colors were beautiful and the stitching was impeccable. Nellie had made one for each of their siblings.

Alvin handed his bride a small box that was wrapped very elegantly. Usually he did his own wrapping in a haphazard way. He purchased this gift at a department store while in Louisville. Nellie looked at Alvin with wonder as she started to slowly open her treasure. It was a gold cross necklace with a small diamond in the center. She surely had hinted enough for it, but it was more beautiful than she ever could have expected.

Daddy was last to open his gift. Nellie and the kids sat a very large box in front of him. Bewildered, he said as he scrunched his face, "I must have been a very good boy for Santy to leave me such a large box." He opened the box, only to find a smaller box, then a smaller one, and so on, until one box remained which was square and flat. "What in the world is going on here? What can this be?" Alvin asked with a confused look on his face. After opening it, he saw all these cut out pictures of large tools. Lying underneath was a gift certificate to a very large hardware store in Louisville. He was going to have the tools he so desperately needed to fix things around the farm. What a surprise. He wasn't expecting this at all.

Soon the living room looked like a bomb had exploded. There seemed to be paper everywhere. In all, everyone was pleased with their gifts. It was such a great family time. Ah, family times meant more to Nellie than anything. There just wasn't anything like it, nothing in the world.

"Will you kids help out and put all the wrappin' paper in this garbage bag while Aunt Debbie and I go and bring in breakfast? Alvin, please stoke both fires." Nellie insisted.

After warming, the rolls and coffee filled the parlor with a great aroma. The kids could hardly put down their gifts to eat, but they managed to get down a roll or two after much coaxing.

Nellie and Debbie went upstairs to change so they could finish preparing the Christmas feast while the rest of the crew dressed. Nellie made the dinner rolls and iced tea while Debbie made the sweet potato casserole. Nellie lit all the candles again. The Baders always ate at noon on Christmas day so everyone could leave to visit the other side of their families.

With all the last minute work to do, time flew by and soon it was eleven o'clock and Uncle Jerry, Aunt Alice and their kids were knocking at the door. They lived about an hour away in Louisville and always had their family celebration after church on Christmas Eve. It was like having two Christmases for them.

"Hey, how are you guys? Glad you could make it," Alvin welcomed. "It's good to see you, Sis," he said as he kissed Alice.

Alvin's sister was tall with beautiful blue eyes. She was a very active woman, and sitting still was not an option for her. She was such a kind and generous person that she would give anyone her last dollar or the shirt off her back, if they needed it. Aunt Alice was also a pretty good cook.

The first door on the left of the entrance was the dining room, and it was used only for company. There was a large front window and a fireplace against the far outside wall. The antique buffet was against the kitchen wall. The matching long dining table sat on a large area rug. A second doorway led into the kitchen. The kids helped set the tables in the dinning room and kitchen while the ladies heated up the food and prepared to serve it.

There was more food than everyone could eat, but that wasn't unusual. The family always stood hand-to-hand around the dining room table while Alvin said grace. Then the children filled their plates. The kids always ate in the kitchen and seemed to do more giggling then eating. Sunnie took this opportunity to tell all her cousins about Mrs. Willow and how rich she seemed to be. Donna was fascinated and wanted to hear more, but the boys were more interested in talking about trains. They kind of ignored Sunnie. This irritated her, and Sunnie shot them a look of frustration.

After cleaning up the dishes, it was time to open more presents with Uncle Jerry, Aunt Alice, Steve and Tim. This gift giving session was a little more low-keyed since money was tight. Even though their gifts were smaller, both the children and adults showed appreciation for each gift. All the adults moved around the room in order to carry on conversations with everyone.

Again the hours flew by quickly. It now was late afternoon and time for everyone to leave. The women quickly helped Nellie clean up a bit. The Baders were sad to see their relatives leave since it would be a long time before they visited again.

Supper was leftovers. Suddenly, from a somewhat silent supper table, Sunnie blurted, "I'm namin' him Skiddles."

"Namin' who Skiddles?" Daddy asked.

"Have you already forgotten, Daddy? What *did* I get for Christmas?" Sunnie said flippantly.

"You should know I'm just tryin' to get a rise out of my new horse owner," Alvin teased with a mischievous smile. Sunnie was definitely Daddy's little girl.

The Baders wound down the evening by playing the Apples to Apples game. It was a family gift from Aunt Alice and Uncle Jerry. Since everyone was tired, the family went to bed around nine-thirty. Even Sunnie was too tuckered out to dream of Mrs. Willow or the horses Sunnie so loved.

Chapter 5

Winter seemed to pass in a flash with only one more light snow, and the first of March came quickly.

As Alvin gathered his wallet and jacket, he said to his daughter, "Sunnie, get your jacket and head out to the truck. We're goin' to town. I need to go to the hardware store and hay market. I know how you like to people watch." Then, before they left, he also spoke to his bride, "Nellie, the boys have gone down to play with Jack. Don't let them stay too long. I'll need their help when we get back."

Nellie nodded and smiled. She walked over and gave Alvin and Sunnie departing hugs and kisses. Then she watched as they made their way out the back door.

Alvin and Sunnie hopped in the truck and headed on down the road. During their journey, they came upon the old Hayfield farm. There seemed to be a lot of construction going on with several bulldozers and other heavy equipment on the property.

"Daddy what's goin' on at Mr. Hayfield's? It looks like they're tearin' it to pieces," Sunnie commented, looking from the farm to her daddy's face with a quizzical expression.

"Oh, that lady from Lexington bought the farm," Alvin replied, sounding disinterested.

Sunnie quickly turned her head to look at Daddy with widened eyes. "Mrs. Willow?" she asked with a flabbergasted tone.

"Well now that you mention it, I do believe that's the name officers John and Adam mentioned," Daddy verified, giving Sunnie a glance. Since Alvin had no interest in this new found information, he was blind to its importance to Sunnie.

"When did you find this out? Why didn't you tell me? You knew she was my new friend!" Sunnie began to rattle, excited and perturbed at the same time.

"Well, I guess she *is* the lady you've been yakin' about. I just totally forgot about it after speakin' to the officers. Apparently she had asked them for information about the community," Alvin told her. Then with apologetic eyes, he said, "I'm sorry Sunnie. I was busy thinkin' of plantin' time."

"Momma thought she might have a horse farm in Lexington. Maybe she's goin' to have one here too! I need to talk to Mr. Perkins. He wants to know all about Mrs. Willow," Sunnie said, even more excited to be going to town now.

"Oh, I'm sure Mr. Perkins already knows. There are no secrets in Pleasureville. Everyone's business is the talk of the town."

Sunnie hoped that Daddy's assumption was not true. She wanted to be the first one to bring the grand news to Mr. Perkins.

A short while later, Daddy pulled up to the hardware store. Sunnie was beside herself with excitement. "I'm goin' to talk to Mr. Perkins. I'll meet you at the hay market. I want *the entire* scoop," she said as she opened the truck door and leaped out.

Sunnie went running into the grocery searching for her friend. Mr. Perkins was sitting at his desk in a small office that sat behind the café out front. He appeared to be working on an order. The back wall had a small chalk board with a schedule on it. There was a window next to the door so Mr. Perkins could look out. The room smelled of papers. It reminded Sunnie of her school rooms.

"There you are, Mr. Perkins!" she said, staring at him with delighted eyes as she stood in his office doorway. "Did you know Mrs. Willow bought the Hayfield farm and is tearin' it up?"

"Oh, she's not tearin' it up, Sunnie," he told her as he looked up from whatever he had been working on. "She's buildin' on it. I hear she's movin' her specialized horse farm here from Lexington."

Sunnie was totally flabbergasted. "I can't believe it! What do you mean by specialized horse farm? What kind of horse farm is that?"

"It's a horse farm that breeds very expensive, high-bred horses; some of which are thoroughbreds. You know.... race horses," he explained.

"You don't say! I can't wait to visit her. Maybe she'll let me play with the horses."

"You don't play with these kinds of horses, Sunnie," Mr. Perkins was quick to inform her while shaking his head. "They are bred, raised, protected and then sold to very rich people who pay high dollars for them."

"All this sounds so complicated," she said with a frown, tapping a finger to her lips.

"Well, it is when you're dealin' with rich people and their horses. It's big business and big money," Mr. Perkins told her.

"Geely whiz! I've got to tell my family and Kim and Kelly."

"That'll keep you busy for a couple of weeks won't it?" Mr. Perkins said with an amused smile, picking up his pen again. He sensed Sunnie was about to dash away. So their conversation would be ending, and he could get back to work.

"You know me too well, Mr. Perkins. I've got to go and meet Daddy at the hay market. Thanks for all the info. You're one of my favorite people," Sunnie babbled as she turned and hurried away.

Ah, and Sunnie was one of Mr. Perkins favorite people too. She always made his day. He knew she earned her name. It was like sunshine and a breath of fresh air when she came around. Besides, Mr. Perkins liked to gossip a bit, and Sunnie was all ears when he had something to talk about.

Daddy had finished loading the last of the hay into the back of his old pick up when Sunnie came running up to him, "I've got *the entire* scoop Daddy. Mrs. Willow is buildin' a specialized horse farm. Mr. Perkins told me all about it. He explained to me about rich people and their horses!" Sunnie told him, hardly stopping to take a breath in between sentences.

Alvin sat on the tailgate with his feet dangling off and patted for Sunnie to sit beside him. He knew it was time to give his daughter some undivided attention. "Well I'm glad you have *the entire* scoop. So you now know about horse farms do you?"

Sitting down where he had indicated and looking up at Daddy with much excitement, Sunnie said, "Kind of.... just how they're cared for and sold to rich people. He said they pay a lot of money to breed their horse with another of high caliber."

"Knowing you, I'll bet it won't take long for you to find out all the particulars," Alvin said with a discerning chuckle.

"Daddy, you and Mr. Perkins know me well," Sunnie admitted with dancing eyes.

"I hear those types of horse barns are more expensive than most people's homes. I reckon they get a fortune for animals like that." Alvin shook his head. "Seems like that farm's goin' up quickly though. I wasn't sure what the harvest would be before talkin' to officers John and Adam, but now it's obvious."

"I wish we could have a farm like that," Sunnie said in a quiet voice, looking down at her dangling feet.

"You know, Sunnie, I imagine a college education is necessary to run such a farmin' business; and college is very expensive," Alvin grumbled.

"Yeah I know," Sunnie said sadly, looking back up at her daddy.

Seeing the dejected look on his little girl's face tugged at Alvin's heartstrings, and he told her, "Look, I know you've always wanted a horse. I love you, and there's nothin' I wouldn't do for my only girl. But you know how I feel about this subject. In life, we can't always get what we want. I know this only too well," he told her, looking down at the ground himself this time. Alvin looked into Sunnie's eyes and said, "Look, there's nothin' wrong with havin' your dreams. Don't let *anyone* take away your dreams." Nodding and smiling, Daddy put his arm around Sunnie and pulled her to him. He held her for a moment before he slid off the tailgate and said, "Well, we'd better be getting' down the road. Let's go." Sunnie jumped down and headed for the cab. Alvin shut the gate and patted it with a tear in his eye. He only hoped he hadn't let his first born down.

As they passed the farm construction again on the way back home, Sunnie just stared, took it all in and dreamed. She didn't want to miss a thing. There were very large pieces of equipment that Sunnie had never seen before. Construction was a new experience for her.

Of course when she got home, she couldn't quit talking to Momma and the boys about what she learned. The boys just shook their heads. They got tired of hearing Sunnie go on and on.

"I guess now we have some more of the Hayfield farm story," Nellie grinned. She knew Sunnie would be on top of every detail. If not her, Mr. Perkins would keep them informed.

Chapter 6

Spring had sprung, and it was time to start planting the early crops. This process involved everyone; that is, any family member who planned on eating. Alvin plowed in the manure and compost. Each child had a specific vegetable to plant. Jonas planted the onion sets, and Ethan planted carrots, both in very straight rows. David was in charge of the white potatoes and Sunnie the sweet potatoes. Nellie liked to make sauerkraut so she put out the cabbage sets. The family worked together the entire weekend to accomplish these important tasks. Of course, Daddy was overseeing and helping everyone. The raspberries and strawberries were established and planted next to the special fence Alvin had made at the garden's edge. The rest of the crops like the pole beans, tomatoes, peppers, cucumbers and watermelon were planted in early May. Luckily, tree planting time was in January or February.

"It's important we do a good job guys. The more careful we plant, the better the harvest. We want to get as much yield as possible," Daddy reminded everyone. Then he went to check on the irrigation system.

Farm work kept the Baders busy, but every time Momma or Daddy went into Pleasureville, Sunnie had to go. Watching the progression of that horse farm was her job. There wasn't a stone turned she didn't know about, or so she thought.

Spring passed quickly for these busy bees, and summer was in full force. Although farm work was the same day after day, there was an occasional variation. Birthdays were one. Nellie tried to make them all very special. It seemed like Sunnie had grown a few inches since last year. She was getting prettier by the minute, but Momma was grateful that her only daughter was still on the immature side. It was peaceful not to worry about boys and other issues parents usually worry about. One Friday night in the middle of June, the family was having supper when Momma said to Sunnie with a grin on her face, "Well my little lady, tomorrow is your birthday. You're goin' to be a big teenager. How does that make you feel?" Momma asked.

Sunnie raised her eyebrows, turned her head to the left and flipped her hair. "Very grown up. Boys, I can boss you all around now," she said hoping to get a rise out of her brothers.

David wasn't going to hold still for this, "I don't *think* so!"

Ethan wasn't happy about that either, "You're not bossin' me around. No way!"

"Boys, cool your heels. Sunnie is joshin' you. She's goin' to do no such thing. We're your bosses," Daddy reinforced as he pointed to Momma and himself.

"I'll cook your favorite dinner tomorrow night, Sunnie. We'll give you your gifts at breakfast if you like," Nellie announced, ignoring the kiddo's usual banter.

The boys wanted to wait until supper to give Sunnie their gift. Ethan and Jonas's personalities were very similar. Sometimes people would comment on how much alike they were. They were thoughtful boys, and talked David into helping them make a jewelry box for Sunnie's birthday. Of course, Alvin had to carefully supervise this project; but the boys did most of the work. It actually turned out to be a nice gift.

Sunnie went to bed early and read for a little while. Reading always made her sleepy, and she thought that would make her birthday come faster.

It soon was Saturday morning, and Daddy didn't go out to the barn. He wanted to wish Sunnie a happy birthday. After all, she was his only girl. He dressed and went to wake up the boys and the birthday girl while Nellie was downstairs cooking bacon, eggs, biscuits and gravy, and pouring juice and coffee. Alvin walked into Sunnie's room. "Happy Birthday, my little teenager. Momma is cookin' your favorite breakfast."

All the boys ran into Sunnie's room, jumped on the bed and started tickling her. "It's time for your birthday spankins'," they announced. Sunnie was compliant and let them have their way. Each one took a soft whack until they counted to thirteen. Sunnie always did the same to them, so fair is fair.

After dressing, the brood went to the breakfast table. Boy, did everything smell good! Sunnie sat at her regular place. She looked down, and there it was, a cup of coffee with a lot of cream. She grinned and took a sip. Yuck, it wasn't exactly what she expected.

"Why that look?" Momma asked.

"I thought it would taste better than this. It always smells sooo good," Sunnie confessed.

"Just as I thought, but you have to drink it. We don't waste food here," Nellie instructed.

Alvin always sang 'Daddy's Little Girl' to his daughter on her birthday....a little off key that is. Alvin cleared his throat. He was compelled to sing to his birthday girl:

"You're the end of the rainbow, my pot of gold.
You're daddy's little girl, to have and to hold.
A precious gem is what you are.
You're mommy's bright and shining star.
You're the spirit of Christmas, the star on the tree.
You're the Easter Bunny to Mommy and me.

You're sugar and spice, and everything
nice.
And you're daddy's little girl."

When Alvin finished, Nellie pulled a package from the back of a cabinet and said with a pleased smile, "Here's your present from Daddy and me."

Sunnie quickly tore open the package. It was a young lady's purse with a wallet that had twenty dollars inside. There also was lip gloss, clear nail polish, a mirror, and a comb inside. She hugged Momma and Daddy. "Thanks bunches, and thanks for the coffee, Momma."

"Sissy, you're gettin' our present at supper," Jonas stated. Then glancing up at Daddy with puppy dog eyes, he asked, "Daddy can you write a song for us too? You never sing to us."

"Well, Jonas," Daddy said, rubbing his chin. "I didn't write that song." Then clearing his throat, he added, "But I'll sure try and have one for you guys on your birthday." Alvin realized he was going to need help with this one. 'Daddy's Little Girl' was a song he learned when his daddy sang it to his sisters. Maybe Anna Rose, the organist at church, would help. She knew a lot about music.

Everyone gobbled down breakfast. Only on special occasions did they have such large meals. "Okay, kids, we need to feed the critters. You know our work is never done," Alvin said while wiping his mouth, sliding back his chair and standing. He rubbed his belly and smiled at Momma in approval of her always delicious cooking. Sunnie was still expected to help with the chores even though it was her birthday. Besides Alvin wanted to distract her while Nellie baked the cake.

Now that the house was empty and quiet, Nellie made a cake in the shape of a horse's head. Nellie had learned cake decorating when she worked part-time at a bakery. She kept the cake hidden until they finished eating supper. Spaghetti

44

and meatballs with parmesan cheese, and garlic bread was Sunnie's favorite.

Momma surprised Sunnie by inviting Kim and Kelly down for the birthday celebration. They had snuck in the front and were sitting at the table when Sunnie came in the back door for supper. The twins had pretty faces, fair skin, and a few freckles on their faces and arms. They had blonde curly hair, bright blue eyes, and pretty teeth. Even though they were twins, their personalities were somewhat different. Kim didn't believe in hearsay, she preferred facts straight from the horse's mouth, so to speak. Kelly was mothering to every living creature. She worried about every stray animal. Both did very well in school. Sunnie loved each of them for their special qualities. She could never choose one over the other. The twins decided they would dress up for the occasion. They wore printed skirts with white lacey blouses. Their mother, Barbara had just bought them new sandals, so they painted their toenails. After all it was important their feet looked good for this occasion.

Sunnie was surprised to see her dear friends. All through supper, Sunnie kept a smile. She couldn't believe that she was now thirteen. When Nellie brought out the cake, Sunnie was glad to see it was a horse's head. It was beautiful. After singing 'Happy Birthday', the boys gave her their gift.

Sunnie opened it very slowly as to antagonize them, "Oh, how beautiful. I love it! Did you all make this?" she asked, holding up the jewelry box in both her hands.

"Yes," they said beaming so proudly.

"Nice! How pretty!" The twins added their approval, nodding with smiles on their faces. They were happy with Sunnie's brothers for being so thoughtful to their friend.

"It's the most beautiful jewelry box I've ever seen. I'll cherish it always," Sunnie said, genuinely touched. So far, this had been the best birthday ever! Sunnie arose from her chair and hugged and kissed each of her brothers. David wiped his kiss off just as she expected.

"Open our present." Kim and Kelly began to chant. They had picked out a horse pin at the Mercantile.

Sunnie took the box from Kelly's hand, peeled back the wrapping, pulled off the lid and gasped. "Look, it's a horse! You girls know just what I like. I love it, and I will wear it all the time!" she promised, pulling it out of the box and pinning it on at once. "I've got just the perfect, safe place for it.... my new jewelry box," she said, touching the top of her gift from the boys again and giving them another glorious smile as well. Sunnie was very happy and content.

Kim explained, "When we saw the pin, we knew we had to get it for you for your birthday. Horses are all you talk about. That....and how much you like Mrs. Willow. So we knew exactly what to get."

Nellie served up cake and ice cream next. Then, after they had finished, Nellie cleared the table, and everyone played Apples to Apples. That seemed to be the game everyone enjoyed, including the adults. It brought about a lot of laughter from all.

Sunnie beamed as she spent time with her friends and family. She was so proud of the horse pin that she wore on her blouse. When they finally finished the game, the birthday girl was disappointed because it meant the evening, and her birthday, was over. Alvin and Sunnie drove the twins back home. She gave them each a final grateful hug and thank-you before she climbed back inside the truck with Daddy and they headed back home.

"Well, did you enjoy your thirteenth birthday?" Daddy asked, smiling and giving her a glance.

"It was the best, Daddy! The best!" Sunnie exclaimed. She settled back in her seat and secretly uttered a little prayer of thanksgiving for all the special people who shared her life. Sunnie felt very blessed.

Chapter 7

It was late summer and harvest time. As with the planting, the whole family was involved with the reaping. A lot of the vegetables would be blanched and put into the freezer that was in the cellar. All of the siblings would take turns pounding the salt into the cabbage in the crock that would brew down there. The smell got pretty rank, but the Baders liked their sauerkraut.

They ate this sauerkraut with Mr. Garrett's homemade smoked sausage, which to the Baders, was what he was famous for. They also enjoyed mashed potatoes made with Pet Milk and real butter.

Alvin and the boys generally helped Mr. Garrett and Jack process the delicious homemade sausage. Like Alvin and his trees, Mr. Garrett had a very special recipe for his delicacy. David's favorite part was squeezing the seasoned meat into the sleeves made of natural pork casings. So the Baders got their share of sausage and the Garretts got their share of sauerkraut.

On one very hot afternoon, Nellie went into town, and of course, Sunnie just had to tag along. While Nellie shopped, Sunnie sat on the bench in front of the grocery, swinging her legs, daydreaming and people watching. She had on a white tank top and blue jean shorts. Her brown hair was pulled up in a pony tail. She was only allowed to wear her flip-flops into town. There just were too many places to cut her feet on the farm.

All at once, Sunnie received a very pleasant surprise. She happened to see Mrs. Willow pull up again at the furniture store and step out of the Rolls. Sunnie leaped to her feet and went running quickly up to her.

Sunnie paid particular notice to Mrs. Willow's summer attire. While most people about town wore their old jeans or coveralls and work boots, Mrs. Willow's casual dress consisted of navy slacks, a white knit top, and white deck shoes. She also had on jewelry: a large diamond, heart necklace and small diamond earrings.

Since Mrs. Willow was tall, Sunnie had to look up at her pretty, aged face. Her curly, salt and pepper hair was still worn in a short bob.

"Hi, Mrs. Willow. I'm so glad to see you," Sunnie told her with a wide, happy smile, waiving her hand at the lady. "I hear you're buildin' a horse farm at Mr. Hayfield's old farm."

"Well hello, Sunnie," Mrs. Willow greeted, returning the girl's smile. She noted that the girl had grown since she had last seen her. "I did remember correctly. Your name is Sunnie; right?"

"Yes," she said as she curtsied.

"I see that news travels fast here," Mrs. Willow commented, looking a bit surprised.

"Yes ma'am. It's a small town," Sunnie reminded her. "Daddy says we know everybody here and sometimes everybody's business," she admitted. Then she added in a more sedate voice with downcast eyes, "Sorry."

"There is no need to be sorry, Sunnie," Mrs. Willow assured her. "I became tired of the bustle in Lexington. Some of those horse farm owners have gotten a bit too big for their britches. A dear friend of mine is in real estate. She informed me about the Hayfield property. I like the quaintness of this small town. The few people that I have met here are kind and helpful…like you," she added to Sunnie's delight. This comment caused Sunnie to look back up at Mrs. Willow and smile. Mrs. Willow continued, "I also love this furniture store." She pointed to the storefront. Then looking Sunnie back in the eye, she smiled, reached to lightly tap the girl's cute, little, freckled nose, and said, "And I like you, Sunnie."

Sunnie giggled and blushed, noticeably pleased.

"Now, if you will excuse me, I need to check on a furniture order and place another one. I have found that this establishment builds the finest pieces," Mrs. Willow shared.

Sunnie blurted, "It's known all over these parts and then some. We have a tree farm. This furniture store buys our trees for wood. We also have the prettiest Christmas trees in the state," she bragged. But trees or furniture wasn't what Sunnie was interested in. She wanted to know all about that horse farm.

"My, my how wonderful. I'm even more excited about my new furniture now that I know where the wood came from," Mrs. Willow told her with a departing grin. Then the lady gracefully walked into the store.

Sunnie made her way over to the window and watched Mrs. Willow with a mountain of questions coming to her mind. She stood in front of the window for a few minutes. Then she decided she might as well pass the time some other way while waiting for the elegant lady. Still somewhat intrigued with Mrs. Willow's big car and driver, Sunnie walked over to the car and tried to make a little conversation with the driver. After all, she never met any strangers. "Do you like drivin' this big car, Mister?" she asked, cocking her head.

"Yes ma'am," he replied, nodding at Sunnie. "Mrs. Willow is a fine employer."

"I'll just bet she is. I would love to work for Mrs. Willow," Sunnie said as she worked her way back over to the window. The gentleman driver just grinned to himself. He kind of had a notion that somehow this girl would work her way into his employer's life.

After some time passed, the pretty lady stepped back out on the walk. Sunnie quickly stopped her and boldly asked, "Mrs. Willow, will you be my friend?"

"Of course I will, Sunnie," Mrs. Willow told her, her lips curving with amusement as she nodded her head. "It would be my pleasure to have you as a friend. It is important that I become a part of this community. You must come visit me some day when the farm is completed. There are many projects to finish, but I'll be moving in very soon. My horses will be shipped thereafter. I hope to be completely settled by late fall. Perhaps I can come to your farm and pick out my Christmas tree. I will need a very large one."

"I'm sure Daddy would help you pick one. We have all kinds and sizes," Sunnie told her. Then quickly changing the subject, she bragged, "I just love horses. I've always wanted one, but Daddy says it's just another mouth to feed. We grow all our food and eat the animals we raise."

"Your father must be a very smart man. That sounds efficient. Growing strong trees good enough for this hand-made furniture is also a wonderful profession," Mrs. Willow praised. "I must meet your family someday soon," she added. Then she paused and looked at her watch. "I really must get back to my estate." She was looking past Sunnie now to her awaiting car and driver.

Before Mrs. Willow could sneak away, she and Sunnie were abruptly interrupted by Pastor Noah, who was heading toward the grocery. "Good mornin', ladies. It's a fine and blessed day. Sunnie, introduce me to your friend here."

"Yes, Pastor Noah," Sunnie politely replied, even though she was not at all happy about this interruption. "This is my new friend, Mrs. Willow. She's buildin' her horse farm on the old Hayfield place." Sunnie still had way too many questions for Mrs. Willow, but not enough time to ask them. She meanly thought to herself, "I wonder how long this blah, blah will go on."

"I'm very glad to meet you, Pastor," Mrs. Willow told him, offering her hand. As the two shook hands, she went on to say, "When I'm settled, maybe I can attend one of your services. I truly love to praise the Lord. I was a member of a large Christian church in Lexington."

"You don't say," Pastor Noah replied, tapping his chin. "Our congregation is rather small and quaint, but we love to welcome visitors. It would be a pleasure to have you, Mrs. Willow. It would give you an opportunity to meet more of the town's people."

"You are absolutely right. I would like that very much," she said with a pleased smile.

"Please excuse me, ladies, I must get to my grocery shopping," Pastor Noah said. Then with a slight bow of his head, he bid them, "Good day."

"Good day," they said in unison. Mrs. Willow stepped off the curve and made her way over to the car door that her driver had opened, but Sunnie stopped her before she could climb inside. She wasn't finished yet.

"What's an estate?" Sunnie asked, drawing Mrs. Willow's attention again.

Although she had numerous things to attend to, Mrs. Willow didn't want to be rude to Sunnie. She enjoyed people's interest in her business, especially this young, eager girl. "Um, let me put it as simply as possible," she said touching her bottom lip with her index finger. "An estate is a large home on a large amount of land."

Sunnie quickly took this information in. Then being a bit forward, she dared to ask, "Do you want my phone number, Mrs. Willow?"

Mrs. Willow was not offended by Sunnie's question. Instead, she graciously stated, "As neighbors, we should exchange numbers. Let us plan on doing that at a later time. Now I really must go," she said again and she bent down and disappeared inside the car.

"Bye, bye," Sunnie said, waving.

Later, getting in the truck, Sunnie kept talking about Mrs. Willow and how she hoped to visit the *estate* soon. Momma sat in the truck without starting it. She wanted to have a quiet conversation about her sons, not Mrs. Willow or horses.

Becoming flustered, Nellie blurted, "Girl, will you hush about that stuff for awhile? I need to go over our plans for the boy's birthdays. You know David's is the last of this month. Ethan and Jonas's are the middle of September."

"Okay, Okay, what about their birthdays?" Sunnie begrudgingly conceded. Then a wild thought struck her and she asked, "By the way, how did you have Jonas on the same date as Ethan's anyway?" Sunnie knew about the birds and bees, but not how to have a baby on another baby's birthday.

"I had nothing to do with it. It had to be God's will. I think they like sharin' their birthdays even though they are two years apart," Nellie stated with a slight smile. Then she rushed on, "Let's get to the birthday plans that we've saved for all year. Since they all like trains so much, we are takin' them to the train museum in New Haven, Kentucky. We hope to spend the night. I think we will go the middle of next month to avoid the heat. Do you want to go or stay with the twins?"

"I don't mind stayin' with Kim and Kelly. I think it's good for you and Daddy to have some special time with my brothers," Sunnie thoughtfully agreed. Suddenly, a light bulb went on, and Sunnie had a great gift idea for the boys' birthdays. "Momma, we need to go into the Mercantile. I saw train hats there. You know, the kind engineers wear. Let's hurry over there. Come on!" She had remembered them from a week ago when her momma had been shopping for school clothes.

"What a great idea. Let's go and see if they still have them," Momma agreed.

The Mercantile only had one floor, but the room was very large. It stocked mostly what the customers requested throughout the year, but it had a small novelty section in the back. Chances are this store would not carry any necessities for Mrs. Willow.

Albert Tillis, better known as Al, owned the store and graduated from high school with Alvin. His daughter, Alexa, had recently returned from college to help run the place. Alexa was about five feet, eight inches with a lean frame and dark blonde hair. She resembled a well dressed sales clerk, the kind you see in big department stores. She was one of the few in the community that had a college degree. It was in business. Alexa was trying very hard to persuade Papa to make some changes she thought might increase sales. "Can I help you, Mrs. Bader?" Alexa asked.

"Yes, Alexa," Nellie answered. "I hear you finished college with a business degree. Al must be very proud of you."

"I hope so, Mrs. Bader. I want to apply what I've learned and get experience here at the Mercantile, and then perhaps spread my wings," Alexa shared.

"Sunnie said she thought you had train engineer hats here," Nellie stated, glancing around.

"Um, I haven't seen them. Just a minute, let me ask Papa. He is in the back checking in stock," Alexa told Nellie, staring away toward the back. After a few minutes, Alexa returned with four hats just like Sunnie described. "Is this what you wanted, Sunnie?" Alexa asked, holding them up.

"That's them. We need three," Sunnie stated with a jovial chuckle in her voice. "Momma don't you think those are perfect?" she asked, pointing.

"I don't think you could get a better gift," Nellie said, briefly turning away from the counter to look at her daughter. "How much, Alexa?" Nellie asked as she sat her purse on the counter.

"They are $5.00 each. That's a total of $15.90. Who are the lucky recipients?" she asked with a friendly smile. The cash register dinged as she rang up the sale.

"The boys' birthdays are comin' up soon. We're takin' them to a train museum in New Haven. Sunnie thought this would fit the occasion," Nellie told her, digging a twenty out of her wallet.

As Alexa took the bill from Mrs. Bader and reached to extract her change from the cash register drawer, she turned towards Sunnie and praised, "What a nice gift, a train-theme birthday. You're a thoughtful sister."

Momma took her change from Alexa's outstretched hand, put the money back in her wallet, smiled, and said, "Thanks, Alexa. We appreciate your efforts. Tell Al we said hi." Placing her wallet back in her purse, she slung it back over her shoulder. "See you again soon. Let's go Sunnie," she said, turning to leave the store. "Remember, little lady, the trip is a surprise so keep your mouth shut." Sunnie assured her momma that 'mum' was the word.

On the way home, although Sunnie took in the 'Willow Farm' project as usual, she was excited to tease her brothers about their gifts. The boys were sitting at the kitchen table playing a game when Sunnie went running in the kitchen door, she hollered to them. "Boys, boys, I got your birthday presents today. Na, na, na, na, nu, nu!"

David asked, "What is it? You can tell me."

"No, tell me," Ethan demanded.

"No, tell me," Jonas followed.

"Never mind, you'll see soon enough. I'm goin' to wrap and hide them. Ha! Ha!"

About then, Alvin walked in from the fields. He thought it was about time to prepare his little men for their birthday gift. "Boys, your birthdays are coming soon. We want to take you *all* someplace special next month, but it's a together gift. I think you will really enjoy this."

"Wow, where are we goin'?" David asked, sitting up tall in his chair with curiosity.

"I know, it's the fair," Ethan guessed.

Nellie smiled and said, "No, it's not the fair, but you will find out soon enough. I will still cook each of you your favorite suppers. I think Sunnie will be stayin' with the twins when we go. She wanted us to have some special time with you guys. Isn't that sweet of her?" Nellie was looking forward to the trip. They didn't leave the farm often, but it meant no cooking or chores.

"Why does Sunnie have to stay at the Garrett's? She's old enough to stay by herself now that she's a *big* teenager," Ethan questioned sarcastically.

Alvin explained, "This is an overnight trip. It would be better for her to stay with the twins. Now I won't tell you anything else about it, so don't ask." Alvin wanted the boys to be full of anticipation and surprise.

"We're goin' to be gone overnight? I can't believe it," David said with a look of awe on his face.

"We're packin' our suitcases and everything?" Ethan questioned excitedly.

"Yep. Now no more questions about this trip. The surprise will come soon enough," Daddy boasted as he raised his hand out to the boys in a stop motion.

"Who's takin' care of the critters while we're gone?" David asked.

Alvin explained that the Garretts would help out as they had helped the Garretts when they were away. That's just how farmers did things.

"Can I start packin' Daddy? I don't want to forget anything I might need." Jonas was trying very hard to rush this trip.

"Not just yet, son. When it is time, Momma will ask each of you what you want to take." Alvin was pretty sure they would all want to bring along their new locomotives, and that was okay with him.

The anticipation had Sunnie's brothers chatting amongst themselves for days, during meals, chores, and play times. They took turns guessing where they might be going. David, Ethan, and Jonas couldn't wait. Their birthdays couldn't come fast enough.

Chapter 8

It was Sunday morning and, as usual, the family went to church. Sitting in their usual spot, Sunnie waved to everyone that entered while waiting for the service to begin. As the large doors swept open once again, Mrs. Willow entered. It seemed as if everyone in the church turned to watch her coming up the aisle, including Nellie. Of course, she was dressed elegantly and was the envy of the other ladies. She had on a black sheath dress. The kind no woman should be without. A gold diamond broach was pinned on her right shoulder. Her large, diamond earrings sparkled. Black and white spectator shoes with a matching clutch were the finishing accessories.

Nellie looked down at her own dress. She felt a little uncomfortable even though her dress was clean and nicely pressed. It seemed so simple compared to Mrs. Willow's attire. Nellie fingered the necklace Alvin had given her for Christmas. She not only had worn it to church today, but she never took it off. Glancing at the rest of her clan, also dressed neat and clean, Nellie told herself that she really didn't have anything to be embarrassed about.

Sunnie stood up and motioned to Mrs. Willow. Her new friend smiled and nodded. When she got to the pew, Sunnie introduced her. "Momma and Daddy, this is my new friend Mrs. Willow."

"Good morning. It is so good to finally meet you," said Mrs. Willow, offering her hand.

"We are the Baders. I'm Alvin," Daddy said, reaching to shake Mrs. Willow's soft hand. Pointing to his bride, he said, "This is my wife, Nellie." Nellie then reached to shake Mrs. Willow's hand. "And these are our sons: David, Ethan and Jonas," Alvin pointed out as Mrs. Willow's eyes strayed to the children. "And of course, you already know Sunnie."

"You have such a lovely family," Mrs. Willow commented giving them a smile.

"Thank you, ma'am," Alvin nodded. "We are proud of them all."

"Come sit by me. I've been tellin' my family all about your farm." Sunnie tried to start up that conversation again.

"Shush, Sunnie. The service is about to begin," Nellie stated as she tugged on Sunnie's arm. She then looked up at their new acquaintance and invited, "Mrs. Willow, please join us."

"Your mother is right. We must give the Lord our undivided attention," Mrs. Willow added as she sat by Sunnie.

After the service, everyone usually chatted outside when the weather permitted. So, as they stood in the bright sunshine with their eyes squinting, Sunnie brazenly asked Mrs. Willow, "Are you goin' to join our church?"

"Well, I suppose that would be the proper thing to do. I like being an active member of a church," Mrs. Willow told her.

Nellie stepped up to Mrs. Willow. "We haven't had a chance to properly welcome you as our new neighbor. We would be very pleased if you would come over for some coffee and cake this afternoon around two o'clock."

"That would be lovely," she accepted with a gracious smile. "What is your address?"

"We are also on Highway 561, just four miles north of your place. Just take a left out of your driveway. Our farm is on the left and the mailbox looks like a birdhouse."

"I look forward to visiting with you. Ciao (chow)!" Mrs. Willow said as she waved and stepped away.

"Ciao," Alvin replied as he waved and watched her head toward her fancy car. Alvin turned and led his family to their old Suburban.

As they were climbing into their car, David asked, "What does chow mean?"

"I believe it means hello or goodbye in Italian," Nellie informed them.

"She's not Italian. She's from Lexington. She told me so," Sunnie informed everyone, thinking she knew all there was to know about Mrs. Willow.

"Perhaps, her ancestors are from Italy. Maybe she speaks Italian. You know we're of German descent. Grandpa Ernest and Grandma Bertha came to America from Germany when they were very young. Momma has some Irish in her," Alvin informed them.

David said, "Now I get it. We all come from somewhere else."

"You got it. That makes you all of Irish and German descent."

"Momma, should you have invited Mrs. Willow over to our old farm? She's so rich and talks so proper and all." Sunnie seemed a little embarrassed.

"Sunnie, you should never be ashamed of us or our farm," she chastised, looking back over her shoulder and flashing her daughter a harsh look. "We do hard, honest work. That's somethin' to be proud of, not ashamed." Nellie said, pretty perturbed.

Sunnie nodded and looked down at her lap in shame. She was uncharacteristically quiet the rest of the drive home. Her intention was never to make her momma upset. Even though the Baders didn't have a lot of money, she wanted badly to fit in with Mrs. Willow so they would be very close friends.

As the family went in the back door, Nellie demanded that the kids change into clean play clothes. "Sunnie, you need to come back to the kitchen and help bake the cake so it can cool. You can ice the cake young lady." Nellie was still a little perturbed with her daughter. "Alvin, take off your tie, but stay dressed as you are. I need you to straighten up the parlor and run the vacuum in there." Nellie's delegating quality was coming out again in full force. Nellie got out her special occasion coffee cups and cake plates that were her mother's wedding china.

Sharply at two o'clock, Mrs. Willow arrived knocking at the front door. She had dressed down for the visit, which Nellie wasn't expecting. She was sure she would still be in her church clothes. Surprisingly, she had on more casual attire consisting of tan khaki pants and a navy-blue top. The jacket that finished her outfit had a multitude of dazzling colors. It could have been worn with anything. Mrs. Willow also had on navy deck shoes.

Alvin let her in. "Welcome, new neighbor. Please come in." Alvin briefly got a glimpse of her car, but David leaned out the door and really got an eye full as Mrs. Willow walked through the large foyer behind the refinished, front door.

Nellie had Sunnie help bring the coffee, milk, and cake into the living room on Emma's serving tray while Alvin escorted Mrs. Willow into the parlor. As all the children hovered around, Nellie couldn't help noticing that beautiful jacket and how it complimented their new neighbor.

"Mrs. Willow, please have a seat. It's good for us to finally get together," Alvin said politely.

As they all were seated, Mrs. Willow took in her surroundings and commented, "What a lovely place you have. You keep it up so well. Nellie, you seem to have a knack for decorating. You really have some fine pieces here."

Dark hardwood embraced all the floors and stairs. As with most old houses, there were nine foot ceilings. Some of the furniture was antique, some was used, and some fairly new.

Nellie timidly said, "Thanks. I enjoy decorating." Nellie tried her best to mingle the pieces so they created inviting warmth in each room. She thought it was important for each room to have a conversation piece which usually was an antique.

Mrs. Willow looked in Alvin's direction and continued, "Alvin, I understand this is a tree farm, and you supplied the wood for the furniture I'm having made."

"Yes, ma'am," he replied, nodding. Then he added, "My father started this tree farm many years ago. I continued and added the Christmas trees."

After Nellie served the coffee, Mrs. Willow took a drink of hers and commented, "Nellie, this coffee is divine. I also love your china. It looks antique."

"Thank you. The coffee is my favorite flavor, half smooth roast and half hazelnut. These dishes were my mother's wedding china."

"That is wonderful! What a magnificent keepsake," Mrs. Willow raved. Then turning to Alvin she stated, "I was telling Sunnie that I must come and get my Christmas tree from you this year. I will need a really large one for my great room. Do you have many large ones?"

"I think we can oblige you," Alvin said as he sipped his coffee. "I've selected a section where I'm lettin' the trees grow tall. We usually supply our state's capital with its tree."

"How exciting that is! Sunnie tells me you grow your own vegetables and also raise animals for meat."

"It's what I was taught as a boy. It is hard work, but it saves money."

"Saving money is very important," Mrs. Willow agreed, drinking more of her tasty coffee. "I'm so impressed with your business and how you operate this farm. Again, I must say you have a very lovely family. You all are very blessed indeed," she genuinely praised.

David blurted out, "You're rich. You don't need to save money, and where did you get that big car?"

"David, that was very rude! Mrs. Willow is our guest," Nellie reprimanded, glaring at him. Looking back at Mrs. Willow, she apologized, "Please excuse our ill-mannered child."

Mrs. Willow nodded as if to forgive. Raising the china up to her lips and swallowing more coffee, she looked David in the eye and explained. "David, I am a bit wealthy, but I did not acquire it instantly. It took years and a *lot* of saving. I could not have gotten where I am today if I had not managed my money well. My car is a result of that endeavor. Therefore, your father is right to carefully save." She turned and looked at Ethan and Jonas as she placed her cup on the table. "Boys, you haven't said much. Maybe your parents can bring you to my horse farm. I would love to show you all around."

"Me too, me too!" Sunnie didn't want to be left out of *that* trip.

"Of course, everyone should come. How about this coming Wednesday? I know you must be very busy, Alvin. What time would be good for you?"

"Nellie, I think we can be done with our chores around two o'clock. Don't you?" he asked, looking in his wife's direction.

"Yes, two is fine. We will look forward to it. Thank you, Mrs. Willow."

"We are neighbors now. Please call me Morgan," she directed. Then she told them, "And when you come for that visit, you might feel more comfortable if you wear your work clothes since we will be touring all the barns."

"As you wish, Morgan. Work clothes it will be," Nellie agreed. She was trying not to stare at their guest. She guessed Morgan to be in her fifties, but in reality, she was in her early sixties. Nellie found this lady to be intriguing and beautiful even with age.

"It's getting late. I really must be going," Morgan said, setting her cup down carefully and standing.

"See you Wednesday, Morgan," Sunnie muttered, springing to her feet.

Nellie scolded Sunnie. "That's Ms. Morgan to you children. Mind your manners now."

Morgan smiled to herself. In the short time she had known the Baders, she could tell that Nellie and Alvin had marvelous parenting skills. She looked at the family and said, "Until then, good day to all."

Everyone stood at the doorway watching and waving as she left. They really couldn't believe what had just transpired. Alvin was thinking to himself, "Imagine her thinking our farm is lovely and well run." Nellie was dazzled by her sophistication and glamour. Sunnie could only dwell on the visit to see the horses. David, Ethan, and Jonas were drooling over the car with a driver.

Nellie glanced up at Alvin. "Well this has definitely been an interesting day."

"Definitely not like our usual run-of-the-mill day. Her farm did go up rather quickly. There seemed to be tons of workers there each time I went by. A lady of her stature can probably get anything done," Alvin added.

"Can you dig that car, and a driver that waits for her? What a deal that is!" David had to get in his two cents worth.

Jonas was beside himself. "I want a car like that!"

Sunnie flippantly attempted to be arrogant. "Well she's *my* new friend and neighbor."

Sunnie was in hot water again. Alvin was disturbed by Sunnie's comment and said, "She is a new neighbor and friend to all of us, Sunnie. Don't you forget that. We must treat her as we do all our neighbors. Just because she has money doesn't make her any different. She apparently has worked very hard to get where she is today. Now, let's drop this rich stuff once and for all. Do I make myself clear?" Alvin demanded as he gave them all a glare. They all nodded yes. "Now go out and play until dinner!" Alvin wanted the children to value Mrs. Willow as a person, not for her money.

Sunnie tried to keep herself occupied for the next few days. She was always offering to help Momma or Daddy, but all she could think about was going to the *estate* and seeing the horses. Visiting with Morgan was like a dream, a fairy tale, or something out of a book. Things like this just didn't happen to everyday people. Where would this new friendship take her? She wondered how many horses there would be. Sunnie's thoughts and dreams kept her awake Tuesday night. She was simply too excited to go right to sleep.

Chapter 9

Jet-black, wooden fences lined the rolling, exquisite, bluegrass pastures of the 'Willow Farm'. The *estate* was overwhelming even from a distance.

Beautiful, large, creek-rock pillars graced the entrance to the farm. Attached to these pillars was a large, two-door, black-iron gate that had the farm's emblem centered on each door. The farm logos were an oval shape containing 'Willow Farm' in the upper portion and a silhouette of a horse at the bottom. The black mailbox at the property's edge also had an iron silhouette of a horse on top. An electric eye opened the gate automatically.

Driving in the Suburban up to the house, on fresh blacktop, seemed to take a lifetime. Aristocrat trees, evenly spaced, flanked the driveway along each side. The scenery became more picturesque the deeper they penetrated the estate.

Already knowing the right answer, Nellie asked, "Are we in the right place, Alvin?" Nellie sounded in awe as she tried to take in everything.

"Yes, we are, my bride. Don't let this place intimidate you," he said, giving her a loving glance. Then he also reminded her, "Morgan is a gracious lady. I don't think we were invited here for her to boast or make us feel uncomfortable."

"I suppose you're right," Nellie agreed, nodding.

"Geely whiz! This is more beautiful than I ever imagined. What a friend I have!" Sunnie sputtered. She could hardly catch her breath. She kept shaking her head.

"Wow, she has enough room for a bunch of kids. Wouldn't it be great to live here?" David said adding his two cents. He just couldn't believe his eyes either.

Ethan and Jonas were speechless. Their mouths dropped. Ethan smacked his cheeks to make sure he was awake.

The driveway formed a circle in front of the large home. A lane also went to the right and disappeared toward the back of the house.

Looking to the left of the main house, they got a glimpse of two smaller houses on the property. Perhaps these were living quarters for the farmhands. Three large horse barns were visible, to the right and behind the house.

Alvin had stopped the car in front of the main house. "Now everyone, listen up," he said, looking back over his shoulder at his children. "Mind your manners. Remember Ms. Morgan is just one of our good neighbors, and don't ask questions. Be sure to say 'please' and 'thank-you'. Most of all, get those expressions off your faces," Alvin carefully instructed. He wanted his family to be mannerly, not out of place.

They slowly emerged from the vehicle with their eyes still soaking up every inch of the house and entrance. The ranch style, main dwelling had an eye-pleasing stone and brick combination exterior with tan trim. Attached to the front entrance was a portico with dark-stained columns at each end. The landscaping around the front of the house and portico was impeccable. The double, front doors were made of oak and stained to match the front columns. They looked to be the product of the well-known furniture store in town.

Alvin took a breath and slowly rang the door bell. They could hear a very loud and low-toned 'ding-dong'. An older, tall gentleman with hair graying at the temples answered the door. He was wearing black pants with a white shirt and black vest. His shoes were shiny black. "Good afternoon. Welcome to the 'Willow Farm'. I trust you are the Bader family?"

"Yes, we are," Alvin stated.

"Mrs. Willow is expecting you. Please follow me into the great room," this gentleman said, sweeping out his arm inviting them to enter.

Jonas whispered to Alvin, "What's a great room?"

He quietly replied, "I'll answer all your questions when we leave."

The enormous foyer had a limestone floor with two large columns flanking the edge of the step down into the great room. Credenzas with marble tops flanked each side of the front doors and were dressed with rustic lamps and beautiful pottery. Off to the left was a business office. To the right was an elegant, open dining room.

Great barely described the room ahead. It was immense. At first glance, there was a huge, stone fireplace that went from floor to ceiling on the opposite, outside wall. The mantel was a thick piece of rustic wood. Large, wooden, cream colored candle holders were grouped at the right on the mantel, and a large sculptured horse was on the left. Centered above the mantel was an oil painting of a handsome man. Below the picture was a large decorative metal box.

To the left of the fireplace was a very long window. To the right were French doors going out to the lanai, and to the right of those doors was the large, open kitchen and breakfast nook.

A beautiful entertainment center encompassed the left wall. It was ornately made of oak and stained a light, reddish brown. To the right of it was a door to what seemed to be the master suite. There was a vaulted ceiling with exposed beams. An iron chandelier hung from the center beam. The walls were a persimmon color. All the woodwork was stained dark. The floor was rustic hardwood with a very large Asian rug of muted earth colors in the center. Two large, beige leather couches and a leather wing-back chair embraced the rug's edge.

"Welcome Baders. It is good to have you here," Mrs. Willow greeted as she walked to the step leading them into the great room.

"Morgan, you have a beautiful home," Nellie smiled as she noticed Morgan's outfit. She was surprised to see her in blue jeans, a knit top and black, cowboy boots. Her slender figure was even more noticeable. The Baders had worn their work clothes just as Mrs. Willow requested.

"Thank you, Nellie. I designed it myself. I had a great architect that was able to bring all my ideas to reality. Please everyone, come and make yourselves at home. Theo is bringing us some tea and crumpets. Children, I hope you like Kool-Aid. I'm so excited that you were able to come and visit."

Sunnie managed to maneuver herself to sit right next to Mrs. Willow on the right sofa. A few moments later, the well dressed man reappeared and sat a tray of drinks and snacks on the large coffee table. "Thank you, Theo. Wait. Before you go, you should meet the Baders," she told him. Then pointing each of them out, she introduced, "This is Mr. and Mrs. Bader, Sunnie, David, Ethan and Jonas."

Theo nodded and said, "It is very nice to meet you." Then centering his attention back on the lady of the house, he asked, "Will there be anything else, Mrs. Willow?"

"No. That is all for now, Theo. Thank you," Mrs. Willow said, giving him an approving smile. Directing her attention to the Baders, she informed them, "Theo is my butler. He's been with me for awhile and runs this household very well. I don't know what I would do without him." Mrs. Willow turned and looked straight at Sunnie. "I know how much you love horses, Sunnie. After we finish our snack, I will take everyone out to the first barn. The remainder of my horses will arrive next week. They will be housed in the third barn."

"We really get to see some horses today?" Sunnie asked, still beside herself.

"Absolutely, I think you will enjoy seeing how we care for these precious creatures. You see, it is my personal belief that the horse is the most elegant and beautiful animal God has ever created. He has served mankind from almost the beginning of time."

"Oh, Ms. Morgan, you took the words right out of my mouth. I feel the same way. I've always wanted one," Sunnie boasted.

"Me and my brothers love trains," Ethan informed her.

Sunnie leaned into Ms. Morgan and whispered, "Momma and Daddy are surprising them, and taking them to the train museum in New Haven. I'm staying with my friends Kim and Kelly." Ms. Willow just nodded so as not to draw attention.

"Sunnie, mind your manners. It's not polite to whisper in front of people." Nellie was quick to scold. She thought it was important to correct her children at the time discipline was needed. This incident only reinforced Morgan's feelings about Nellie and Alvin's parenting.

Sunnie then pulled back from Mrs. Willow, sat up straight and folded her hands in her lap. She did not want to embarrass Momma or Daddy.

Happy to see that her daughter was minding her manners again, Nellie told her host, "This is excellent tea, Morgan. Where did you find it? I haven't seen any like it at the grocery."

"I order it from a specialty tea shop in Lexington. I like a variety of teas, don't you? I could order some for you as well, if you like," she graciously offered.

"Thank you, but I'm more that way with my coffee. Mr. Perkins orders my favorite flavors. He is able to get it at a good price and passes the savin's onto me. No one else in town seems to care for flavored coffee. Perhaps he could do the same for you. He always goes the extra mile for his customers."

"I will definitely keep that in mind. That would save me time and money," Morgan said in a appreciative tone.

Sunnie quickly started a conversation with Mrs. Willow, occupying her with a thousand questions. So while all the chatter was transpiring, Nellie tried to nonchalantly take in the décor of the great room and the open kitchen area. There were so many beautiful pieces sitting around the room and on the large, sofa table. In the right back corner were two upholstered chairs. Their fabric was deep cream with small crimson horseshoes and saddles. An antique table was sandwiched between them. The lamp atop looked old as well. A ceramic horse was a whatnot placed on the top left corner. The whole area appeared to be for reading.

The kitchen contained cherry cabinets. From a distance, the counter tops seemed to be black. The floors appeared to be light hardwood. The walls were painted celery green. Although the house seemed to have a simple design, each room was large and decorated grandly. Nellie didn't want to stare too long and draw attention to her nosiness. Although Morgan did notice, she didn't mind. She was fond of Nellie's décor as well.

Sunnie's next question brought Nellie to attention again. "So when do we get to see your horses?" She heard her daughter ask.

"Sunnie, don't be so rude!" Nellie reprimanded her again, silencing the girl for the first time in several moments.

"It is OK, Nellie. I know Sunnie is anxious. Now if everyone is finished with their tea and snacks, I will take you all out to the barn," Morgan told them, to Sunnie's delight.

Sunnie practically leapt to her feet. As they were escorted out the doors of the great room, Nellie again noticed the beautiful kitchen which seemed to contain every bell and whistle needed for cooking. The covered lanai was the length of the great room. Flag-stone was inlaid on the floor. There was a built-in grill of stone at the right end that wrapped around in an 'L' shape towards the backyard. On the left was a rod iron dining set with beautiful fresh flowers in the center. Nellie noticed the variegated colored roses, daisies, and lilacs that were delicately placed in a crystal vase. Above this setting was a ceiling fan. Adjacent were some wicker chairs and a table which held an unusual lamp made of real horse shoes. Atop the table was a horse figurine with a small clock in its side belly.

The back lawn was embraced by numerous gardens with various species of plants, shrubs, flowers, and ornamental trees. A concrete walk flanked by bricks went from the lanai to a black wooden gate. The yard was encased by the same black fencing as the pastures. The gate had the farm's logo on the front and back. Beyond the gate was blacktop that curved to the left toward two smaller houses and to the right up to the barns.

It was apparent the barns were designed to be similar. All were white metal with green trim and green tin roofs. To the left of the first barn was a smaller white building. It had three golf carts inside. Flanking both sides of the barn was roofing giving the stall windows shade. The barn had large, green double doors.

Morgan had been walking slightly ahead of the Baders. As she kept walking, she turned to them and said, "I must apologize for not introducing you to my farm manager, Cole, and his assistant, Emilio. They have gone into Lexington to purchase some equipment."

Morgan reached to slide open the barn doors. The inside area was immense. It was also immaculately clean. Three long-hanging, lighted-fans were spread evenly in the center of the ceiling. A heater was mounted at the front, left of the ceiling. There were twelve stalls in all, six to each side. Each large stall was constructed of rough wood with aluminum grills at the top. Each door contained a horse's nameplate at midpoint. The nameplates were varnished, light-colored wood with black lettering. The stalls were also brightly lit. Bales of straw were stacked at each end of the barn with wall phones and fire extinguishers. The center left side of the barn contained a large stainless steel sink with a garden hose, bins of grain, and shelves containing grooming supplies, ointments, medicines, etc. At the center right side was a small tack room containing everything necessary for riding horses. The barn's center flooring was an unusual material.

Alvin, of course, was curious. "What is this floor made of?"

"We use recycled tires. It is soft to walk on making it easy on the hoofs and can easily be cleaned," Morgan explained.

"Well if that don't beat all. I guess I've seen everything now." Alvin said with amazement. "I noticed a heater. You heat these barns?"

"Yes Alvin, but only enough to take out the bitter cold. We want the animals to get their winter coats so they can exercise in the pastures. Now, let us meet the horses," she said with a smile. Then looking at Sunnie, David, Ethan and Jonas, she instructed, "Children, you may pet the horses, but I ask you to approach them slowly and pet gently so as not to startle them."

Morgan went from stall to stall, and Sunnie was, of course, the first up to each. As Sunnie reached to touch each horse, she gently called its name and stroked the nose ever so carefully. Sunnie was praying to herself that some day she would have a horse all her own. She told each one that it was the prettiest horse there ever was, and how much she loved him or her. There were twelve in all, but Sunnie took her time with each one. Alvin or Nellie had to prod her along so the remaining family could see these lovely creatures. Sunnie's extreme interest and enthusiasm was very pleasing to Morgan. She had secret plans for Sunnie brewing in her sharp, old mind.

When they got to the other end of the first barn, the doors were open. To the left and a short distance away was another barn looking similar, but slightly different from the first. Morgan explained, "This left barn is used for breeding. The third, right barn is like this first and will house the remaining horses that arrive next week." The barns formed a circle area containing fine, soft wood shavings. "Please follow me." Morgan escorted the Baders directly across from the doors of the first barn. "This small barn and fenced area you see straight ahead is where we keep the goats."

"You have goats too?" Sunnie shouted. Goats were another favorite animal of hers.

"Yes. They have a calming affect on the horses and are an important part of this business," Morgan explained as she pointed to another area. "To the left of this third barn you can see our training corral. We also have a particular horse whisperer that we sometimes use for the more difficult horses."

Sunnie jumped in, "What's a horse whisperer?"

"Well Sunnie, a horse whisperer is a man who uses special calming techniques which are not at all like the usual training. Again, he's only called in for the horses with difficult temperaments," she explained with a slight smile. Then she pointed and directed. "Please carefully walk behind here with me. In this area behind our goats, you can see two horse trailers which are for transporting the horses. These trailers contain three slanted stalls in the back and living quarters in the front. Sometimes we must go a great distance in them."

Alvin spoke up, "I had no idea these trailers had livin' quarters. I guess this beats goin' to expensive motels."

"Yes, and in some areas, there isn't even a motel. Whoever is transporting the horses need not worry about finding a place to sleep," Morgan added. Then glancing around at everyone, she asked, "Are there any other questions?"

"I have plenty, but that would take all day," Sunnie confessed, turning her upper body side to side. She could have stayed forever and talked about horses.

"Sunnie, in time, your questions will all be answered," Morgan told her with a widening smile. "I do hope everyone enjoyed my little tour."

"That's an understatement!" Sunnie exclaimed. She would never forget this adventure. She was smiling from ear to ear and brimming with excitement.

Nellie laughed and said, "The poor twins, Mr. Perkins and everyone else will have to listen endlessly about this visit." This statement only reinforced Morgan's interest in Sunnie.

"Thanks for the tour. We really appreciate it. It was so much fun for us all," Alvin told her. He had enjoyed himself and learned a few high-tech things such as rubber tire floors and horse trailers.

"Yes, Morgan. It was kind of you to take time for us," Nellie added.

"It was my pleasure," Morgan told them. Then after a slight pause, she said, "I had a thought. Alvin and Nellie, would it be possible for Sunnie to come back Saturday? She seems to have such a great love of horses. I really would like to teach her more about these creatures."

"Oh boy, can I? Momma, Daddy, is it Okay?" Sunnie was quick to question with wide-eyed enthusiasm. This slightly immature teenager was beside herself. She couldn't believe her ears. It was like a dream come true.

"I hate for her to impose," Nellie replied, not wanting her daughter to become a nuisance.

"Quite the contrary, it is no imposition. I assure you. I asked because I would be delighted," Morgan said with a smile.

"Well, if it's alright with you. What time do we need to bring her?" Nellie asked.

"No need. I will have my driver pick her up at ten AM." Morgan was quick to offer, but she also prudently asked, "Will this give her time for breakfast and her chores?"

"Yes, ten is okay," Alvin gave his approval with a nod. Then he added, "Speakin' of chores, we need to be gettin' back to our farm."

Morgan pointed, "Let me escort everyone to the door."

The family passed, once again, through the garden, lanai, and great room. Nellie quickly took in more of the scenery. She liked decorating and enjoyed seeing other styles.

Standing before the front door, Morgan said, "Sunnie, I will see you Saturday morning. Wear your work clothes again. I don't want you to ruin your nice things."

"I can't wait, Ms. Morgan! I just can't wait!" Sunnie squealed, bouncing up and down.

"Sunnie, this won't be play time," Morgan cautioned. "There is much to learn and a lot of work to do," she told her, fighting back a smile at the girl's obvious enthusiasm. She was looking forward to having Sunnie come back.

"I won't forget, Ms Morgan. I'll be rarin' to go and ready to learn."

"Well, goodbye all. It has been a great pleasure having you," Morgan told them, sweeping open the grand front doors.

The Baders all waved as they went out the doors towards their vehicle. After getting into the Suburban, they had looks of amazement on their faces.

"Can you believe it? I get to go back. My friend wants me to come back. Wow!" Sunnie said as she clapped her hands with joy.

"Sunnie, try to contain yourself, and don't badger everyone with this matter. You'll make a nuisance of yourself," Alvin demanded.

"I'll try Daddy. I will try, but I need to tell the twins and Mr. Perkins just a little about our visit today."

"Only just a little, mind you. I won't have you wearin' people out with this?" Alvin warned.

"Yes sir. I promise," Sunnie said with a nod, but she was already trying to figure out how to condense everything she needed to tell everyone.

"This was fun, but I still like trains better," David stated.

When they got home, Sunnie was allowed to call the twins and tell them about the visit and how Mrs. Willow wanted her back at the horse farm. Kim and Kelly loved Sunnie, and they seemed happy for her. But they were hoping it didn't take away from their time with her.

The excitement was almost too much for Sunnie to bear. It was three long days for Sunnie. They seemed to be endless, but Saturday *did* arrive.

Chapter 10

Mrs. Willow's driver arrived promptly at ten AM. He knocked at the door and Sunnie ran to answer it as fast as she could. "The car awaits you, young lady," the driver said, offering his hand.

"Momma, Daddy, this *young lady* is going now," Sunnie called back to them with an ear-to-ear smile. She had never thought of herself as a young lady until now. "Kisses and hugs, I'll be back later," she said as she bolted out the front door, leaving it wide open. The screen door slammed behind her.

Alvin walked to the door from the kitchen, opened the screen door, and called out to Sunnie, "Mind your manners, and don't forget to say 'please' and 'thank you'."

The boys came running and gathered at the front door with Daddy. They were a little envious that Sunnie got to ride in that big expensive car. This time, the gentleman was dressed in tan pants with a short sleeve tan shirt and no hat. He escorted Sunnie to the vehicle. The driver was short and heavy and sported a salt and pepper mustache with a go-tee beard. He was smiling as he opened the back door and helped her in. Sunnie flashed a toothy smile back at him, feeling like a real special person...a queen. What a ride this was going to be, what a ride indeed.

It really wasn't far to her friend's farm, but the journey seemed to take forever. Sunnie took advantage of this time to check out every inch of the car. The vehicle had a new-car smell and was roomy inside. The seats and door panels were beige leather, which felt soft and smelled of richness. The steering wheel was made of deep, rich wood as was the dash. There was a phone in the rear seat console. The Rolls Royce must have been new because it didn't seem to have any wear.

"Thanks for pickin' me up, mister. What is your name?"

"My name is Oliver," he told her looking back at her in the rearview mirror. "You may call me Oliver."

"Oliver, I like that name, and you can call me Sunnie. Everyone does. I'm Ms. Morgan's new friend and neighbor. She needs my help with the horses," she proudly told him, looking at his big blue eyes in the mirror.

"Yes ma'am. She informed me that I would be picking you up on all your visits," he confirmed, nodding.

Sunnie's mind raced, and she squirmed in her seat. That must mean she would be coming back. Oh, this friendship was going to be more than she ever expected, much more.

"Oliver, what do you do when you're not driving this car?"

"Miss Sunnie, I tend to the gardening."

"You did a good job on the pretty flowers around Ms. Morgan's house," Sunnie complemented.

"Thank you. I love to garden," he replied. They settled into silence for the rest of the drive.

Arriving at the 'Willow Farm', the driver pulled up to the portico. Sunnie fumbled with the door handle and tried to get out. "Sunnie, I will help you out. It is my job," Oliver informed her. He then got out of the car and came around to the right, back door. Opening the door, he held out his hand to Sunnie. When she took it, she was grinning with a smile wider than the ocean. He smiled back and helped this charming young girl out of the car. Then Oliver escorted Sunnie to the front door and rang the bell for her. His first thoughts about Sunnie back by the furniture store seemed to be coming true. She was becoming a part of Mrs. Morgan's life.

"Thank you, Oliver. I enjoyed my ride very much."

"Yes ma'am. It was my pleasure," he stated nodding his head as Theo answered the door. Sunnie didn't know how to take Theo. He had a British accent and was the first butler she had ever met. Sunnie noticed him more carefully. She wanted to become his friend too. Theo was dressed similar as before with black slacks, white short-sleeve dress shirt and a black vest. He was tall and lean, and his graying temples set off his black hair. Sunnie had guessed he was a bit younger than Mrs. Willow. There was something about him that Sunnie couldn't put her finger on. Although he was a servant, he must have been more like family. Hopefully she would get this straightened out.

"Mrs. Willow is expecting you. Please follow me to her office. Mrs. Willow, Ms. Bader has arrived," Theo announced as he gently bowed toward Sunnie.

"Theo, you can call me Sunnie. Everyone does." She smiled and patted herself on the chest.

"Yes, ma'am," he replied, nodding. He led her off to the left of the impressive foyer at the doorway to a warm, bold office.

Glass French doors led into the office. Covering the entire back wall were mahogany book shelves that had large drawers and doors at the bottom. Some of the shelves contained different statuettes of horses and other items pertaining to horses along with numerous books. The walls were painted a buttercup yellow with a hardwood floor giving a certain warmth and contrast to the mahogany furniture.

Mrs. Willow was sitting behind the beautiful, ornate desk in the center of the room in a burgundy leather, executive, high-top chair. An antique, brass lamp rested on the right side of this desk. A laptop computer was placed open on top along with a black business phone that sat to the left. The desk was graced with a couple of horse artifacts.

An expensive, oriental rug with shades of burgundy, green and cream was placed under the desk area. An antique table decorated with a reading lamp, porcelain horse, and a brass riding hat sat centered at the large, arched window on the outside wall. A wingback chair with gingham fabric of cream and burgundy sat left of the table. Tall mahogany shutters reached up to the arch and were pushed open. On the right wall, a wide curio cabinet sat full of whatnots and antiques. It contained a light that gleamed through the glass shelves making each piece noticeable. To the left of the doors, against the foyer wall, was a Queen Anne chest with a marble top. It was decorated with a lamp that had a beaded shade and more horse paraphernalia. The walls had a couple of oil paintings of various horses, one of which was above the chest. The paintings had lights above them.

"Sunnie, come in and sit down. I'm glad you are here. Sunnie was a little intimidated by the formal room and the formality of Ms. Morgan. She seemed to be all business, not at all like the other encounters. "I have been checking our website. I wanted to make sure it was updated correctly. Do you have a computer at home?"

"Yes. It's in Momma and Daddy's bedroom," Sunnie replied as she had a seat in the wingback chair which faced the desk and sat at the rug's edge. The chair was covered in buttercup fabric with burgundy and green stripes. It was apparently a guest chair. "Daddy uses our computer for the tree business. David and I can use it for our homework too, but we are not allowed to play on it. Daddy doesn't want his files ruined."

"I can understand that. I know you are familiar with a tree and animal farm, but this farm is a fairly complicated business. Here we board, breed, buy and sell Thoroughbreds and Tennessee Walking horses. Each type of horse is pastured separately. We also provide veterinary, training, and photo services to our clients. Now young lady, just how interested are you in learning about horse farming?" she asked, placing her elbows on the arms of her chair and folding her hands in front of her. Mrs. Willow had a serious look about her.

"If it's okay with you, I want to learn anything you will teach me. I've always wanted to be around horses," Sunnie sheepishly replied.

"That is good," Morgan praised, a slight smile appearing on her face. "You definitely will get your fill here. You see, I never had any children to teach my business to. My husband, Andrew, passed away two years ago. It is a good thing I have surrounded myself with knowledgeable people. You are so young and enthusiastic about horses. I thought I could take you under my wing, but I do feel it is important to get your parents' approval. I also thought perhaps you could stay with me when your parents take your brothers on their trip to the museum. Would you like that?"

"Do you really mean it? I can stay here for a few days? Are you sayin' I will be here a lot?" Sunnie asked, sitting up tall in her seat, excitement glowing in her eyes.

"If you are serious about horses, it would be my pleasure, Sunnie," Morgan said, her smile widening. Sunnie's enthusiasm always made her day. Morgan grew more serious again, as she cautioned, "Again, your parents must approve. It is imperative you keep your grades up and do what is expected of you at your farm. You must never neglect any of these to be here with me. Is that understood?"

"I understand, Ms. Morgan. This experience is too important to me. I promise to do good," Sunnie's head was nodding up and down.

"The correct grammar is 'I promise to do *well*'," Morgan corrected.

"Yes ma'am. The right word is 'well'," Sunnie agreed, excitement still oozing out of her. Ms. Morgan spoke with dignity and sophistication. Sunnie wanted to be just like her. She made a mental note to pay special attention so she could mimic her. Learning to speak properly could be part of her many lessons.

"May I call your parents now?" Ms. Morgan asked.

Sunnie gave her number to Morgan one digit at a time. Morgan dialed as she called the numbers out. While waiting for an answer, she wrote the number down in her address book.

This highly dignified woman could be persuasive in a gentle, kind manner. Nellie answered the phone. Morgan politely asked permission to have Sunnie spend a few hours each week and learn about horses. She also explained about not having any children of her own and wanting to take Sunnie under her wing. Morgan also asked if Sunnie could stay while they were away. Nellie replied by saying she would discuss this with Alvin and get back to her shortly.

Sunnie had many questions for Ms. Morgan. What did her parents say? Was it okay? She was scared they would say no.

"Your mother will discuss this matter with your father when he returns from the barn. In the interim, you can come with me," Morgan said as she stood up from her desk chair. "I want to make sure the third barn is prepared for the horses that will arrive Monday."

As the girls walked through the great room, Sunnie's eyes were drawn to the large painting above the mantel. "Is that a picture of your Andrew?"

"Yes it is. I adored that man. I will always love and miss him greatly," she told Sunnie with a pained expression on her face.

Meanwhile, at the Bader farm, Nellie was pondering the conversation she had just had with Mrs. Willow. She didn't know what to think. She didn't want Sunnie to be in the way. Why would such a wealthy lady want Sunnie around? Sunnie was her baby girl, and she didn't want to lose her to all the glamour and wealth. She waited for Alvin to come back from the barn.

Alvin finally came into the house rattling, "I finally got those stalls fixed. They are much sturdier. The boys were a big help today. I can't wait to surprise them for their birthdays." When he looked up at Nellie he said, "My, you have a strange look on your face. What's goin' on?"

"I got a call from Morgan earlier. It seems she wants Sunnie to learn the horse business, kind of take her under her wing. She also wanted to know if Sunnie could stay with her when we take the boys to the museum. I feel as though she's tryin' to take our daughter away from us. I just don't know what to think about all this."

Alvin twisted his mouth and rubbed his chin. "Um, things seem to be happenin' *kind* of fast with that friendship....I must admit. I do recall a conversation I had with John down at the station a few days ago. He was tellin' me that Morgan was the pillar of her community, gave a lot to charities and such. He said she and her farm manager were very well liked....I believe his name is Cole. Word has it, she may be wealthy, but doesn't put on airs, so to speak. John said she's a real classy and refined gal, kind and generous."

Nellie's face had a frown with a curious look. "How did he find all this out?"

"Since she's new to our area, he wanted to get some info on her." Alvin nodded. "Seems he called another officer he knows in Lexington. Looks as though she is as she seems to be and then some. Besides she's a God-fearin' woman," Alvin smiled. "I like her....she seems genuine. I really don't think her intention is to take Sunnie away from us. I think she just wants to give Sunnie an opportunity to learn about somethin' she obviously loves. We'll monitor the situation, but I think it will be okay. I don't think there is cause for us to worry, Nellie."

"Well, if you're sure. I guess it's okay. I told her we would discuss it and call her back. Here's her number. You call."

Alvin dialed the number and Theo answered. The girls were out in the barns so Alvin left a message for Morgan to return his call. Hanging up the phone, Alvin remembered. "Oh, I forgot to tell you. Anna Rose has written a new song for the boys. They seemed a little jealous about Sunnie bein' the only girl who has her own special song. I'm supposed to go by the church after supper so she can teach it to me. Maybe you can come along. I think Sunnie is old enough to hold down the fort here for an hour or so. The boys are always good."

"Sure we can do that. That will be an added special gift. It's very thoughtful of you to have a special song written just for them," she commented, giving him an approving smile. She loved Alvin very much, and it was special little things like this that he would do that made Nellie remember all the more why she married him.

Morgan and Sunnie walked slowly through the first barn. Morgan knew Sunnie would want to see all the horses again. Sunnie made a point to call each horse by name and wave to each. She could have stayed at each stall and talked to them, but she could see that Ms. Morgan had an agenda. As Morgan saw more of Sunnie's enthusiasm, she was both touched and amused. It only confirmed her decision to take Sunnie as her apprentice.

The girls walked into the second barn. This building was arranged differently. It had two offices to the left and one on the right. There was an 'L' shaped area that attached to the right office which had a door at each end. The path went to the left, around it and out the back of the barn.

Curious as usual, Sunnie wanted to know why this barn was different, and why it had offices. Morgan explained carefully. "This first left office is shared by the farm's manager and me. The gentleman that designs the farm's website uses it as well. The second office is used for buying, selling, and boarding horses. My top farmhand uses it. The right office is used for clients who pay for breeding. This 'L' shaped section at the other end has a staging area where horses are introduced. It also contains the breeding area. Only the handlers and guiders are allowed in these areas when the breeding transpires. Even I do not go in there at this time. You are never to go beyond these doors when they are closed and you hear noises. The clients are, however, allowed to watch from the office here on the right, but not all do. After all, they pay a fee of $10,000-$25,000 per event. I trust being on a farm, you understand how animals breed."

Sunnie frowned, "Don't they know to do this in private? It's so embarrassin'."

Morgan explained, "Animals have the sense God has given them. Therefore, when the time is right, they only follow nature's course. Humans, on the other hand, know how personal and private this matter is. It is God's gift for only those who are married. That is something you must always remember." Morgan smiled, placing her arm around Sunnie and patting her arm. "You see, you have already had your first lesson with many to come, and the correct word is embarrassing."

Sunnie knew it really wasn't her first. She had questions that were much more important than courting lessons. She asked her first one now. "Why does it cost so much to breed horses? That's more money than I'll ever make."

"You never know what the future holds. Perhaps you will be wealthy one day. You see, these spectacular creatures come from the finest blood lines. This is another lesson for you. Now let us check out my third barn before returning to the house."

As they approached the back door a tall man appeared. Dark blonde hair barely showed beneath his worn cowboy hat. His face sported a dark tan. He looked to be about twenty-five, although in actuality, he was only nineteen. His attire consisted of a light blue jean shirt with the 'Willow Farm' logo on the right pocket and dark blue jean pants. His brown boots had quite a bit of wear to them. "I see we have a visitor, Ms. Morgan."

Morgan looked at Sunnie and introduced the man. "This is my manager and right-hand man, Cole. Cole, this is my new friend Sunnie."

He spoke with a deep voice as he tipped his hat, "Ma'am, it's nice to meet you. Welcome to the 'Willow Farm'."

"Nice to meet you too. I love it here. Ms. Morgan says I will be here to learn about horses."

"Yes, she has explained that to me. As I understand it, I may be somewhat involved with that. Now if you will excuse me, I am expecting someone in the office. I will see you again soon, young lady." He tipped his hat again and walked toward the offices.

Morgan went on to explain to Sunnie, "In spite of his youth, Cole has enormous experience and expertise with horses. He was raised around these beautiful creatures and knows just about everything there is to know. Cole is a hard worker and has taught me a thing or two about horses. I could not run this farm without him, especially since my Andrew's passing."

Although this gentleman was older, Sunnie thought he was handsome. Her mind was entangled with so much. They approached the next building. The third barn was just as immaculate as the first. Soon it would be full of beautiful horses as well.

Morgan went from stall to stall inspecting every detail. "Everything seems to be in order here," she said both to herself and to Sunnie. Then turning her full attention to the girl, she said, "Sunnie, I've been thinking. I feel it would be appropriate for each barn to have a specific name. I want you in charge of naming them. You can give them to me on your next visit. Would you like this challenge?"

"You want me to be in charge of namin' the barns?" Sunnie asked, her face lighting up.

"Yes, it is your first project."

"I'll do my best Ms. Morgan. I really need to get on my thinkin' cap for this one."

Morgan smiled and gently cupped her hand under Sunnie's chin. "The correct word is '*thinking*' not 'thinkin'. You must always pronounce words correctly. If you expect people in this business to take you seriously, you must speak properly. Now let us return to the house."

There was so much to learn, even for a fresh teenager, but Sunnie believed she was up for it. Again, she made some mental notes about speaking correctly. After all, she had learned the proper way in school, but got into the habit of speaking like most country folk.

As they entered the French doors of the great room, Theo greeted them. "There is a message for you on your desk."

"Thank you. Sunnie, follow me." As Sunnie tagged along behind Ms. Morgan, this flabbergasted girl took in every detail of the great room again. It seemed bigger than life. Sunnie's attention was brought back to Ms. Morgan when she heard her friend say, "The message is from your parents. Please take a seat."

"What do they want? What did they say about me stayin'…I mean staying here?" Sunnie asked, apprehensively taking a seat.

"It seems your parents want me to call," Morgan shared as she picked up the phone. She dialed as Sunnie sat and watched with anticipation. "Alvin, how is your day going? That is good. Did you and Nellie have time to discuss my request?"

Sunnie couldn't hear what Daddy was saying, only Ms. Morgan saying 'yes' here and 'I understand perfectly' there. She started to bite her nails, which was a first. Then she sat on her sweaty hands.

"She is sitting here in my office. I will speak with her and have Oliver bring her home shortly. It was nice speaking with you. Please give Nellie and the boys my best. Ciao."

"What did he say? Can I come back? He wasn't mad was he?" Sunnie stood up and shot questions at Morgan before she could barely lower the phone.

"Slow down, Sunnie, slow down," Morgan requested, shaking her hand palm down at her. "Sit back down. Your father and mother gave their approval to my request with some stipulations. You are allowed to stay here while they travel, and you may spend a few hours a week here as well. They are in agreement that you must keep up your grades and your chores, and above all, you are not to slight your family and friends in any way. Is this understood?"

This lovely young girl was filled with joy. So much so, that she almost wet her pants. Sunnie stood up and smacked herself in the face. "Holy moley," she shouted. Sunnie simply couldn't believe Ms. Morgan wanting her to stay and her parents allowing it. Was she dreaming? Should she pinch herself? She could hardly catch her breath.

"Sunnie, your face is flushed. Do you want some water? Are you alright?" Ms. Morgan asked with concern, pouring a glass of water for her apprentice, and handing it across the desk. It was one of Theo's chores to keep cold water on his employer's desk.

"Uh huh. I just can't believe it, that's all!" Sunnie exclaimed, taking the glass and gulping down the water as she sat back down.

"You're a business woman now, so believe it. I want to explain a few things before Oliver takes you back home. Over the last few days, I have developed a modus operandi for your visits that will benefit us both. I hope you will approve."

"A who-da-whata?"

"This is another lesson. Modus operandi is Latin and it means 'method of doing something'. Let me explain. I have developed a plan for your visits. Most of all, I want you to enjoy yourself. You are young, and your mind is like a sponge. It will absorb any information that is given. You see, this is a productive sector, which is complicated to run. I employ experienced people that love the horse business. You already love horses, but you lack experience. Let me reiterate, there is much for you to learn here. I want your time here to consist of three functions. One: I want you to meet my employees and learn from the expertise of each. Two: Watch and, at times, assist them. Three: you will also spend some time with me."

"Does this mean I will work for you?"

"Not so much in the beginning. Besides you are too young to work and be paid. Think of it as an apprentice program. Also, remember you have school, which is very important. I know there is much to learn, but I really want you to enjoy yourself. Although this is serious business, we do occasionally joke with one another. We have a lot of respect for each other, and work well together. We are like a close family here. Some of my employees live in the other houses, and all of them get personal time off. You know how hard it is to operate your farm with the trees and animals. This is hard work as well. Do you think you are up for it? Will you hold up your end of this bargain?"

"Yes ma'am! Yes, Ms. Morgan," Sunnie confirmed, bouncing in the chair. Her new teacher answered a pondering she had had earlier about Theo. That's why he was different. Not only was he a servant, but he was family as well.

"Good!" Morgan approved with a smile. "I will see you again when your parents leave town." Morgan buzzed Oliver and escorted Sunnie to the door. She patted Sunnie on the cheek and said, "Ciao."

Sunnie curtsied, "Ciao to you, and thanks for everything, Ms. Morgan." She remembered to speak properly."

Morgan hung at the door. While watching Sunnie leave, she had a smile on her face and a warmth in her heart that had not been there since Andrew had passed. She missed him terribly. Andrew had been the love of her life, but she was too busy to date again. She really didn't want any part of it. Perhaps this child would help fill the void somehow. She put her heart into this farm and now into Sunnie. This delightful teenage girl had a way of melting it.

Morgan gazed into the sky with deep thoughts, remembering when she and Andrew built the business from scratch. Because they could not have children, they put their energy into a shared love of horses. Since they already had a couple of these animals, they decided they could make money from something they both had knowledge of and enjoyed. And so the business slowly grew into the business she was currently running. As she continued to stare into heaven, she said a little prayer. "Thank you, Lord, for bringing this delightful child into my life."

Chapter 11

Sunnie arrived back at her house. She was so grateful that her parents had agreed to let her spend time at the 'Willow Farm'. At lunch, she described her first project to Momma and Daddy. After a long line of thank-yous and promises to keep up her grades and chores, Sunnie suddenly felt exhausted and excused herself. It had been a big day, so she went to her room to reminisce and dwell on her first project. She lay on her bed with a pad and a pencil in hand and commenced to write names for the barns, but before long, she fell fast asleep.

Still sitting at the kitchen table, the boys were feeling a little slighted and jealous. They weren't interested in horses, but in trains. David had to get in his two cents worth. "Sunnie gets to have all the fun. We never get to do anything excitin'."

Jonas added, "Yeah, we're special too. We do most of the work around here. She only gets to play."

Alvin felt it was time to inform the boys about the trip for their birthdays. "Listen up, boys. First….," he said, holding up his index finger. "Sunnie isn't goin' to the 'Willow Farm' to play. It is a complicated business. She's goin' to learn….kinda like school. Think of it as a specialty school. Besides we have a great surprise for your birthdays. Now, who likes trains?"

"We do, we do, we do," they yelled in unison.

"Next week we are takin' you to the train museum in New Haven. We are goin' to spend the night and also take you all out to eat for supper and breakfast. So what do you say? Do you guys want to go?"

"Oh boy, I can't wait," David shouted, rubbing his hands together.

"Me either," Ethan agreed while wiggling in his seat.

"Me too! When do we leave?" Jonas added with his eyes lit up like a Christmas tree.

"We're leavin' next Friday as soon as you get home from school. We'll stop for supper on the way. Momma has made a reservation at a small motel near that area. Early next mornin', we will eat a good breakfast and go to the train museum. We'll come home in the afternoon. The Garretts will take care of things here. Now, tell me who's goin to have *fun, fun?*" Alvin could see the joy in his sons' faces. It was good that they could enjoy something they loved too.

"Yeah, we are, we are," they shouted.

"Thanks, Momma and Daddy." David said. He was usually the first of the boys to say thanks. Getting up from the table, he gave both his mom and dad a hug and then added, "I'm callin' Jack and telling him about our trip, but I know Jack will be more interested in Sunnie's horse stories. He loves horses too." Ethan and Jonas also pushed back their chairs and leapt to their feet, rushing to bestow hugs on their parents and emphatically thank them.

"We're goin' to have more fun than Sunnie does at that horse school," Jonas added.

"You bet, my little brother," David agreed, playfully hooking an arm around his neck. As they walked away, he gushed, "We'll have a blast. Besides, we've never stayed at a motel before, and we don't get to eat out much." The brothers went out the back kitchen door to play for awhile.

Ethan realized something. "Guess what we won't have to do that Saturday morning?"

They all three looked at each other and said in unison, "Chores!" They commenced to giggling their heads off.

Still secluded in her room, Sunnie finally woke up after a long nap and looked at her pad. So far she had written: Mane, Tail, Saddle, and Bridle. After thinking a bit, she wrote more ideas: Stallion, L-o-o-o-v-e Barn (she laughed to herself thinking of the breeding room), Mare, Bluegrass, and Kentucky. She had an idea. Perhaps she could get a lot of info from the internet, but she needed Daddy's permission to go this route. In the meantime, she looked in the dictionary. Under 'horse' there was reference to the word 'equine'. She then looked up 'equine': an adjective - *to or like a horse*. So she added Equine to the list. This would take a lot more brainstorming. Maybe her thinking cap would work better with a full stomach. She had been in her room all afternoon. Sunnie just realized she was very hungry and the smell of chicken frying was creeping upstairs.

It was Jonas' turn to set the table and help with the dishes. The children had to take turns with this chore, but with four of them, it wasn't too bad. Besides they liked having Momma one-on-one. The conversations, at times, became very interesting. Nellie and Alvin always wanted the kids to feel free to ask any questions they liked. The couple didn't want them to get incorrect information from other sources.

Nellie had cooked a grand supper: fried chicken, mashed potatoes and gravy, and green beans. She also served cottage cheese, iced tea, and milk. The boys were filled with excitement for their special trip. Sunnie was more than beside herself from her experience. Alvin and Nellie were just glad the children had the chance to do something each would enjoy.

At the table, the boys told Sunnie about their trip. She acted surprised and happy for them. Sunnie asked Daddy if she could do some internet research on horses after supper. He agreed and warned her about the sites she should not visit. Alvin informed the kids that he and Momma had an errand to run after supper. Sunnie and the boys were given rules on behavior and such. The doors had to be locked up tight and some lights kept on. They also were instructed not to let anyone into the house.

Alvin helped his bride clean up after supper so they could be on their way. As their parents left, the children promised to behave. Sunnie went back upstairs to the computer in her parent's room. After logging on, she did a search on horses, horse farms, horse breeding, and such. She then came across another word to add to the list: 'Equestrian': noun or adjective – *a horse rider or the riding of horses*. After printing and reading much of her research, she added other words to her list. She rewrote them on a clean piece of paper. The list contained the following:

Mane

Tail

Saddle

Bridle

Stallion

L-o-o-o-v-e

Mare

Bluegrass

Kentucky

Equine

Equestrian

Paddock
Breeders
Halter
Bits
Chestnut
Bay

Sunnie stared at and contemplated each word putting them together in numerous ways. Thinking to herself, she wrote down three words: Mare, Stallion, Foal

Not bad she thought. This covers the basis of what the farm was about. Barn #1 could be Mare, Barn #2-Stallion, and Barn #3-Foal. Finally a light bulb came on. She thought to herself. "What about Kentucky Bluegrass Equestrian or maybe Equine." She wrote them out together a few spaces down: Kentucky Bluegrass Equestrian or Equine

"That's it," she shouted out loud. Sunnie even surprised herself coming up with such sophisticated and important words. "Ms. Morgan will like them I'm sure," she said again out loud. "I still like the L-o-o-o-v-e Barn. Ha! Ha!" She smiled thinking of herself as a very important person with an important project, which she felt she had accomplished very well. She also liked the first three names, so she decided to give both sets to Ms. Morgan and Cole.

It seemed like it would be an eternity until next Friday afternoon. Sunnie turned off the computer and went into her room to gather the clothes she wanted to pack. She had new boots which would be appropriate. After all, she saw Ms. Morgan and Cole in them. They also wore blue jeans. So this excited teenage girl picked out a couple of her better jeans and tops to pack. She happened to think that Ms. Morgan would probably be going to church. Sunnie also picked out her favorite dress and shoes. Momma and Daddy had given her a small suitcase the year before for her birthday since she often spent the night with the twins. Ready to be more than prepared, she packed her outfits along with underwear and PJs into the suitcase. She was now ready to go!

Sunnie went downstairs and fixed a snack for everyone. She explained that baths and PJs were in order after they finished. Sunnie liked being the last in the bathroom. She could take her time and soak awhile using the bathing products she got from her cousins for Christmas. It made her feel grown-up and pretty.

In the meantime, Alvin and Nellie had arrived at the church. As they went in the side door, they could hear the piano playing. They walked down the hall and turned left into the large fellowship hall. This was the room that was used for the church bazaars, craft shops, receptions, and such. Tables and stacking chairs were at the far, end wall. To the right of them was the piano facing into the room. The right wall had a door leading into a very small kitchen which smelled of metal and a hint of cooking oil.

Anna Rose was rehearsing the new song she wrote for Alvin to sing to the boys on their birthday. The tune was a catchy one with an uplifting beat. Nellie's eye fell upon Anna Rose before she looked up from the piano. Anna wasn't dressed to the nines as usual. Nellie was so used to seeing Anna at church services wearing fancy dresses and accessories that matched her attire so perfectly. However, dressed more casually, Anna was still a strikingly attractive woman. Her skin was simply beautiful. Her hair was a shiny silver color which was a little straighter than normal.

Anna Rose looked up and waved them over to the piano. "I hope you like this tune and the words. Let me play it for you. I titled it 'Boys from Heaven'."

After singing it twice in her lovely, lyrical voice, Anna asked Alvin to sing along. They continued until Alvin got the tune and words down. Nellie could see a slight smirk on Anna's face. To Nellie, this confirmed that Alvin was a little tone deaf. Alvin knew how to read music so now he could take it home and practice a few times; and boy, did he need practice.

"Alvin, it sounds as though you have this song down pat," Anna Rose said as she winked at Nellie. "Just be sure to practice a few times before you sing it," Anna instructed.

"Thanks for all your effort. I didn't know how to come up with a song unless I got some professional help. I couldn't have done it without you, Anna Rose," he said with a grateful smile.

Anna explained that the pleasure was all hers, and that it gave her a chance to be a little creative. She usually only played the hymns and songs the pastor would select for each Sunday's service and special events.

On the way home, Alvin tried to sing the song from memory. "Not too bad my dear," Nellie said with a smirk. "I believe you've *got* it," she added. "I think we should do something special for Anna Rose. After all, it did take a lot of her time. What do you think, Alvin?" Nellie asked.

"We could send her flowers, but they don't last very long. I would like to give her something that would remind her of this song. What if I made her a decorative, wooden box? I could trim it in copper or brass. I'm sure I could get the hinges and a latch at the hardware store. I should draw it up first. Maybe you could help with the design."

"That's a great idea! Perhaps we can work on it each day while the children are at school. We definitely need to put a lot of thought and effort into it. It should be unique and very special," Nellie suggested. She loved doing crafty projects.

Sunday came, and the Baders sat in the same pew as usual. Sunnie kept watching the door in hopes that Ms. Morgan would come. Morgan finally walked through the doors; and of course, Sunnie waved her forward. Sunnie patted the pew to show Ms. Morgan where to sit. When she sat down next to her apprentice, Sunnie wiggled in her seat and started to tell her, "Ms. Morgan, I worked on the project you gave me; and I've come up with some great names."

"Shh....Sunnie," Morgan said, holding a finger to her lips. "That will keep until Friday. You are in the Lord's house now. You need to remember to give Him your undivided attention." She then looked up at Nellie and winked, hoping she hadn't stepped on any toes.

"Yes, Ms. Morgan," Sunnie agreed. A bit shamed she downcast her eyes. She still was very eager to share her delightful news with Morgan, but she realized that now was not the time or place. She would just have to continue to be patient and wait until next Friday. The wait would be excruciatingly long for Sunnie.

Morgan saw the disappointment on Sunnie's face. She hated to hush the child. Sunnie's enthusiasm always brightened Morgan's days. Morgan Willow was a spiritual woman in spite of the occasional crudeness of her business. She and Andrew had attended a very large, Christian church in Lexington. They felt that God had blessed them in many ways. Therefore, it was important to be a servant to Him. Morgan was still unsure why God hadn't given her and Andrew children, but she tried to accept His will even though it was so hard to do. Having Sunnie in her life now, made accepting this fate much easier. Morgan reached to squeeze Sunnie's hand. As she closed her eyes, she said a silent prayer of thanksgiving to the Lord that this delightful child was now a part of her life.

Chapter 12

Nellie always liked to organize the children's clothes and supplies for the first day of school. Sunnie was a big help because she wanted to be prepared. She was looking forward to being in classes with Kim and Kelly. The boys were also excited. They enjoyed being with friends that they didn't see often and learning new things. They knew that it was important to get an education in case they were to ever take over Daddy's tree farm.

The two schools in Pleasureville were Henry county schools. Therefore, the Baders were lucky that the school bus stopped right at the end of their driveway. The first day of school was a great day. The school and its rooms had the unique scent of books, papers and chalk.

The twins and Sunnie were gathered in the hall before the morning bell rang with friends they only saw at school. They were all trying to quickly catch up on their summer events. Sunnie, of course, was blabbing about her upcoming stay with Ms. Morgan to everyone. Most of the girls were intrigued and a little jealous. They finally excused themselves for class. As Sunnie glanced over to Kim and Kelly, they appeared to have worried looks on their faces.

"What's wrong with you two?" Sunnie asked. "What's those looks on your faces about?"

The twins looked at each other with concern and Kim confessed, "You're not going to have time for us anymore, especially now that school's started."

Sunnie explained that Ms. Morgan and her parents had given her strict orders not to let her chores, grades or friendships slide. She promised to make an effort to spend quality time with them. This information was somewhat comforting to Kim and Kelly, but they still had reservations. Although the twins were well liked at school because of their friendliness, Sunnie was their best girl friend of all.

The Bader kids thought the first week of school took forever to pass. During this week, Alvin and Nellie come up with a great design for Anna Rose's box and had collected the supplies for their project.

It was finally Friday morning. At breakfast, the Bader children were eating faster than usual as if this surely would help the day go by faster. Alvin stood up from the breakfast table and loudly cleared his throat. Everyone looked up at him. Sunnie and Momma knew it was time for him to perform. Alvin proceeded to proudly sing, a little off key, his special song to the boys.

Boys From Heaven
"You boys are special to Momma and
Dad.

For when each arrived, we were very glad to have three to carry on the family name.

Who knows if someday you may have fame?
When you all grow up, someday you may be, a boyfriend, a husband, perhaps a Daddy.

There's so much to teach a boy about life.
Much more than playing with trains or flying a kite.

Each of you are special. Your own person be.

You're loved more than you know by
Momma and me.
Please always be there for Sis and each other,
And feel blessed you have a sister and two
brothers.
Be strong, have courage, stand up for
what is right.
Be proud men carrying God's light."

"Daddy, did you write that song for us?" David
inquired as he stared at Daddy with amazement.
"I liked it a lot," boasted Ethan while grinning from ear
to ear.
"Me too! Now we have a song too, sissy!" Jonas
shouted with a really big smile.
"Boys, Ms. Anna Rose, the organist at church, helped
me. She knows so much about music and all. I gave her some
thoughts about how Momma and I feel about you guys. Each
one of you has your own special personality. You boys mean
the world to us. We wouldn't trade you all for anything."
"Thanks Daddy," they said in unison.
Sunnie said excitedly, "David, Ethan, Jonas, here are
your birthday gifts from me. I thought of them all on my
own." Sunnie had found some boxes in the storage room and
wrapped the gifts in newspaper. Each boy was tearing and rip-
ping paper as fast as he could. "Wait! Slow down! You all
need to open them at the same time," Sunnie demanded.
"Wow, it's an engineer's hat. Guys, we can wear them
to the museum," David shouted.
"I'm an engineer now," Ethan exclaimed.
"We can all pretend to be engineers," Jonas added.
"Thanks, Sunnie. It was so thoughtful of you," David
said while giving the hat a good once over. Momma had
drilled the children often about showing appreciation.
"Thanks, Sissy," Jonas added as he placed the hat on
his head.

"Yeah. Thanks bunches," Ethan said as he also put his hat on and marched around the kitchen making woo-woo sounds.

"You're welcome. I really enjoyed *pickin'....uh picking....them* out. I saw the hats at the Mercantile and asked Momma to take me there." Sunnie was trying to become more aware of her grammar.

As the children got up from the table to leave for school, Nellie said, "I've made all the arrangements. I'm packin' our things for the trip today. I'll also pack us some drinks in our little cooler and some snacks to have while we ride. When you come home from school, we'll head down the road. I just want to make sure Sunnie is on her way first. Oh Alvin, Morgan has offered us a cell phone to take with us. She said she would feel a lot better if she could get in touch with us. The driver will leave it and a couple of phone numbers when he picks up Sunnie."

"That's a good idea. I'll have to admit that I would feel better havin' it. I would like to call Sunnie when we get there and when we start back home. What a kind gesture," Alvin stated.

The school day passed surprisingly fast. The principal and PTA thought it was good for the children to learn how important it was to help people less fortunate. So the school developed a project time for selected charity work. The older classes would be singing at retirement homes in Louisville. The younger classes were gathering can goods and toiletries. The youngest children were drawing pictures for the retirement home. It did help to keep the Bader children's minds off the excitement of their upcoming events. Luckily, they had not been given homework for the first weekend of school.

When she arrived home from school, Sunnie ran in the door and up to her room to double check her suitcase. She brought it to the front door and made sure the door was opened wide so she could watch for Oliver.

Alvin had packed the Suburban after Nellie gathered the snacks and prepared the cooler. Momma and Daddy were almost as excited as the boys about their trip, but they were also somewhat apprehensive about leaving Sunnie at the 'Willow Farm'. This was the first time the family had been apart. It had been a very long time since they had gone away from the farm; only a few day trips to the Kentucky State Fair in Louisville. Vacations did not occur often when there were farm animals to care for and much work to do.

Hopefully Alvin, Nellie, and their sons would enjoy being away from their daily chores. They had earned a vacation from all that hard work. There was no doubt that Sunnie would be in hog heaven.

Chapter 13

Sunnie saw Oliver pull up in the car, so she ran to kiss her family goodbye. Oliver got out of the car and came up to the porch to gather Sunnie's luggage. He nodded at the Baders and escorted his passenger to the car. Sunnie smiled and waved at everyone.

Nellie turned to Alvin and laid her head upon his chest with tears in her eyes. There was still something tugging at her heart strings over this new friendship. Plus, her daughter was growing up right before her eyes. This situation was much different than Sunnie staying with the twins. Perhaps it was because the rest of the family would be out of town. Alvin hugged Nellie and patted her on the back. "She'll be okay, my bride. We need to let her grow up a little."

"Let's go Alvin. Maybe the trip will help keep my mind off of it," Nellie said while locking the front door and heading toward the back door.

Alvin called to the boys, and they dashed out of the house. Then the Baders got into the Suburban and headed to New Haven for their own grand adventure.

While driving to the 'Willow Farm', Sunnie reviewed her project and hoped Ms. Morgan would be pleased. Oliver had expected Sunnie to talk his ear off, so he enjoyed the unusual quiet.

Oliver helped Sunnie to the door. Theo welcomed her as he took the suitcase and walked her to the carefully prepared guest room. After showing her the bath and other amenities, he offered her a snack, but Sunnie was too excited to eat. Theo explained that Mrs. Willow was expecting her in the office at the second barn. Sunnie was to bring her finished project. Sunnie ran up to the first barn and walked quickly through while waving to everyone. She tried to calm down and slowly walked into the barn with the offices where Ms. Morgan and Cole were awaiting her.

The office was small with a large window by the door which faced out into the barn for viewing the day's activities. The walls were a light gray with a few black and white horse pictures scattered about. The small desk faced into the room from the left. Morgan's chair was black leather. There were two guest chairs facing the desk.

"It's good to see you Sunnie. Come sit down. By the way, how is school going?" Cole greeted.

"Hello, Cole and Ms. Morgan. School has been great. We've been workin'...uh...working on a project for charity. I also finished the project you gave me, Ms. Morgan."

"Charity work is good for the soul. I had my favorites in Lexington," Morgan commented. Then she encouraged with a smile and said, "Please show Cole and me the names you have created for our new barns."

Sunnie had pretty good penmanship. She had written out two copies and gave one to Ms. Morgan and one to Cole. This little apprentice sat tensely in the chair with her hands sweating.

"This is some list you have, little lady. I'm impressed," Cole stated, flashing a pleased grin.

Sunnie giggled at Cole's praise, noticing how his smile brightened his face and made him even more handsome. She heard Ms. Morgan speaking which brought Sunnie back to reality. "I can see you have put a lot of thought into this." Sunnie looked her new friend in the eye as she heard her add, "Please carefully explain your conclusions to us."

"Well, I tried to think of things that pertain to horses or things used by horses. I still kind of like the word 'Lo-o-o-v-e' for this barn." She laughed. "After all, we all l-o-o-o-v-e horses and they must lo-o-o-v-e each other when they are here."

Cole and Morgan snickered a little, but tried not to show it. Morgan explained, "I understand your thinking, but I really don't feel it would be appropriate considering our clientele. Please continue."

"The first set of names, I like very much. 'Mare, Stallion, and Foal' kind of sums up what this farm is about, but I was afraid they would be too simple. Then, a light bulb went off in my head. I finally came up with 'Kentucky, Bluegrass, Equestrian or Equine'....whichever. I thought they suited Ms. Morgan's personality more. Do you like any of these or should I come up with more names?"

"Cole, what do you think?" she asked glancing his way. "This is going to be a hard decision." Ms. Morgan had already made up her mind, but this was a group decision.

"I like them equally," Cole replied. Then turning his attention to Sunnie again, he told her, "You did a great job with these."

Cole's acclamation made Sunnie's day. She chuckled and looked down at her toes, slightly embarrassed.

Cole found Sunnie to be very cute and a refreshing addition to the 'Willow Farm'. He wanted to help her learn as much as possible. Along these same lines, he said, "I do have a thought on making a decision. If we use the first set of names, employees and clients may get confused as to what we are talking about. For example: Get the mare from the Stallion barn. But if I said, bring me the mare from the Kentucky or Equestrian barn. It would be much less confusing." Pausing and pulling on the end of his chin, he asked, "Does any of this make sense?"

"You make some excellent points, Cole," Morgan told him. She was always pleased with this wise young man's input. Looking back at her young protégé, Morgan asked, "Sunnie, what do you think?" Morgan wanted Sunnie to feel like she had made the final decision.

"I think the second set of names suits this farm best. They are sophisticated like Ms. Morgan." Sunnie nodded as she smiled up at her new friend.

"Cole, are you in agreement?" she asked, glancing his way again.

"Yes ma'am," he confirmed, raising and lowering his head.

"Then it is official," she proclaimed, tapping her desktop. "Barn #1 will be named Kentucky, Barn #2-Bluegrass, and Barn #3 will be Equestrian." Turning her full attention to her farm manager, she instructed, "Cole, please order the name plates and have them placed above the doors at both ends of each barn." Looking toward Sunnie, she commended with a wide, satisfied smile, "Sunnie you did an excellent job and put a lot of thought into this project. I am very pleased with this." Pausing, and reaching into a drawer, she pulled forth a pamphlet. "Here is some literature for you to read about nutrition for our horses. This can be complicated, so read the material carefully. I don't expect you to remember everything all at once. Experience will be your best teacher. Your next project is to find out about the horses we are boarding, their names and everything we do to care for them. I want you to take notes and refer to them often. We will go over your findings tomorrow afternoon. A good place to start is in the next office. Emilio can assist you. He is Cole's assistant."

"I can't wait to get started," Sunnie proclaimed, springing from her chair. "See you guys later." This project also gave Sunnie a continuance of feeling important. So, with a giant smile on her face, she marched into the next office with pad and pencil and commenced to introduce herself to Emilio and ask a thousand questions.

As the two horse experts overheard Sunnie's enthusiasm, Cole said, "Mrs. Willow, having Sunnie here is going to put sunshine into this place. It was a good decision. I like her a lot. She has great potential. I'm going to enjoy teaching her. It reminds me of when I was young growing up around horses."

"I was counting on you feeling this way, Cole," she said with a bittersweet smile. "You and she are going to be my family. Although you work for me, I feel as though you are like a son. You have helped me so much with the old farm and the building of this one. We have a great deal of respect for one another. You are a wonderful young man, Cole."

"Thank you Mrs. Willow. I think you are a grand lady," he told her, his eyes warm with affection.

Morgan smiled from ear to ear. "Well, I guess we are even." Sliding back her desk chair and rising, she said, "Now, I must go up to the house and make a few calls and give Theo instructions for dinner. Please join us." Cole occasionally had dinner in the main house with his employer. Most of these meals were business dinners. They could discuss the employees, their performances, and needed training without them overhearing.

Sunnie noticed that the short, dark-haired, dark-skinned gentleman she was now meeting with talked with some kind of accent. Being her usual nosy self, she questioned him about how he spoke and where was he from. Emilio was a polite and gentle soul. He explained that he was originally from Mexico (he pronounced it Me-i-co) and had met Mrs. Willow five years ago at the Keeneland racetrack in Lexington. Sunnie had not met many people with accents and none from other countries. The wheels in her mind were already turning. She decided to give him the third degree about Mexico. How exciting it would be to tell her classmates and friends about Emilio and his country. This would be great for geography class.

Emilio gave Sunnie a notebook that Ms. Morgan wanted her to keep all her notes and lessons in. He took her to the Equestrian barn and introduced her to each of the spectacular creatures housed there. Sunnie proceeded to write down all the information Emilio gave her on each boarded horse. All she could think of was how to build a relationship with each one. She wanted these animals to trust her as they did their caretakers. Emilio instructed Sunnie to come back to his office tomorrow morning at nine AM, and he would go over the material and answer more questions.

Sunnie made a mental note to make sure and set the alarm as she headed back to the house. When she entered the great room, the smell coming from the kitchen was wonderful. Momma was a great cook, creating everything from scratch. Sunnie thought she would still love to have a butler to do some of the work for her.

Morgan instructed Sunnie to wash up for supper and told her that they would be eating in the kitchen tonight. While washing up, she couldn't help thinking of how awesome it would be to sink into that wonderful bed and gaze around the room at all the beautiful things in it. Still having trouble believing all this was real and not a dream, she looked up into the mirror while drying her hands. She pinched her cheek and grinned back at herself. Sunnie folded her hands and looked up to heaven and gave thanks for this special opportunity. In spite of her youthfulness, Sunnie loved Jesus very much. After all, look how he had blessed her.

After sitting down at the table, Morgan proceeded to say grace. As Theo placed all the food on the table, Sunnie graciously thanked him. "Theo, this looks and smells so good. Aren't you eating with us?"

"Thank you for the compliment, young lady, but I usually eat with Oliver."

Even though Sunnie was only thirteen, she noticed again that Cole was quite good looking. She was young, but not blind.

The conversation at the table was mostly about business and schedules. Sunnie was a curious being and had to know where everyone on the farm lived. Morgan explained that Theo and Oliver had complete living quarters downstairs. Cole lived with Emilio in the first house out back, and the remaining help lived in the second, smaller house. Morgan also talked briefly about how they went to the races at Churchill Downs and Keeneland.

"Perhaps you can attend the next Derby with me, Sunnie. We usually have many friends that have horses racing," Morgan invited.

"We always watch the races on Derby day with friends, the Garretts. It's been a dream of mine to be there one day," Sunnie admitted. She mentally noted that she needed to be sure and pinch herself again before bed and hoped she wouldn't wake up from this gigantic dream she was experiencing at the 'Willow Farm'.

"Well there is much for you to do and learn before May. Let us cross that bridge when we get to it," Morgan said, not wanting Sunnie to get ahead of herself.

Cole excused himself to attend to a few things before going to his house. When Sunnie was sure he was out of ear shot, she said to Ms. Morgan, "Boy, Ms. Morgan, Cole is a real looker, isn't he?" There was a grin on Sunnie's face and a twinkle in her eye.

"Yes, he is a nice looking young man," Morgan acknowledged. Then she added, "But he is like a son to me. His parents have passed on, and he came highly recommended to me. We actually learn a lot from each other. Although he is employed by me, we are family. I also couldn't do without Theo and Oliver. Theo is very good at running a household. He knew I needed a driver and recommended Oliver. They both came from England."

"Really? Now I know someone from Mexico and two people from England. That's a first for me. I haven't been out of Kentucky much, let alone to another country. I hope they don't mind me asking about their countries. It will be a great geography lesson for me."

"You are right, Sunnie. They all have fascinating backgrounds. I am sure they would be delighted to enlighten you. You must tell them about your wonderful family and what it is like to live on a tree farm that has been handed down from your grandparents," she encouraged.

"Daddy said his parents came here from Germany when they were very young. Just imagine what it is like to live in another country," she said with imaginative eyes full of wonder.

"I'm sure my staff would be interested to know that your grandparents came from Germany. After all, we do live in the greatest country in the world. No wonder so many come here to live. I'd say this farm is a good cross section of this world," Morgan added.

"Yes, it seems so. I will enjoy exchanging stories with them. Ms. Morgan, I just love being here," Sunnie told her with a happy laugh. "There's so much to learn from so many people. Thanks again for inviting me."

"The pleasure is all ours, young lady," Morgan said with a delighted twinkle in her eye. Pushing back her chair and standing, she told Sunnie, "Now, I must work on some upcoming projects before retiring. There are books in your room if you choose to read. Perhaps it would be best if you study your notes. You should go to sleep early for we rise at five AM here."

"Yes ma'am. I will set the alarm," Sunnie told her, also pushing back her chair and standing. Starting away toward her guest room, she added, "See you in the morning, Ms. Morgan. I'll be dressed and ready to go."

Morgan couldn't help but walk over and give Sunnie a hug and a kiss on the forehead. As she watched Sunnie head off to bed, she thought how this was going to be good for her farm, and good for her heart.

Sunnie took a nice long bath and snuggled into the plush, comfortable bed. She took Morgan's suggestion and studied her notes for awhile, but within a half hour, she was fast asleep.

Sunnie was up sharply at five, dressed and ready to go. After breakfast, she helped with many of the chores, such as cleaning a few stalls. Promptly at nine AM, she reported to Emilio. Even surprising herself, she had memorized every detail given to her about each horse.

"Excelente, Señorita Sunnie. You did very well," Emilio praised with a surprised smile.

"Emilio, what did you just say?" Sunnie questioned, wrinkling her nose.

"Excellent, Miss Sunnie," he replied. Then he readily offered with his charming Hispanic accent. "If you wish, I can teach you how to speak Spanish."

"Oh I would love that!" Sunnie cooed. "Would you?"

"Sí, señorita, sí. Sí means yes in English."

Sunnie knew that she and Emilio would become good friends. There was something special about his demeanor that drew her to him.

The next two days were intense, but fun. Every once-in-awhile, Sunnie would catch herself staring at Cole. This was her first crush, but she couldn't let on. There was too much to learn and too much to do.

It was Sunday around three PM when the Baders passed the 'Willow Farm'. "I hope Sunnie's weekend went okay," Nellie stated, staring out the window.

"We can share our stories when we all get home," said Alvin. He had missed his little sunshine girl. So when they got home, he called Morgan immediately.

"How was your trip? Did the boys like the train museum?" Morgan asked.

"I can't tell you how much fun we had. It's hard for us farmers to get away, so it was a real treat."

"I think Sunnie also enjoyed herself; but the training was, at times, intense. She is such a delightful girl, Alvin. My manager, Cole, and I feel this is a good fit. We really need someone who is willing to learn every aspect of this business. Please let me know if Sunnie fails to do what is expected at home and school. There will be opportunities for you and her friends to visit so you will understand what she is learning."

"Thanks, Morgan. It really was gracious of you to let her come," Alvin told her. Then he requested Morgan to send his missed little girl home.

"I will have Oliver escort her promptly. Ciao." Morgan stepped out on the lanai. Spying Sunnie, she called to her, "Sunnie, gather your things. It is time for Oliver to take you home." As Sunnie drew near, she shared, "I think your family had a really enjoyable trip."

"Oh, I'm so glad, because I would feel guilty having had such a great weekend. Thank you, Ms. Morgan. Just let me know when I need to come back."

Sunnie was delighted to hear Morgan say, "Perhaps next Saturday afternoon would be nice. I will call your parents mid-week."

Sunnie walked into the house with Morgan. She went into the guest room and gathered her things. Then she met Morgan and Oliver outside. After Morgan had instructed Oliver to gather the cell phone from the Baders, she gave Sunnie a hug and sent her on her way.

When Sunnie got home, she discovered that the boys were excited about their trip to the train museum. For once, they were going on and on about everything they saw: the motel, how fun it was to order in the restaurant, and all the many model trains they saw. The best part of the trip was that they all took a short ride on a real train. Sunnie's brothers wore their engineer caps the whole trip, even to bed. She was gracious and kind and listened, but occasionally interrupted with her own schedule of events. For the first time, she finally got a taste of her own medicine. The boys just couldn't shut up. They blabbered on and on about their trip until bedtime.

Chapter 14

As overwhelming and difficult as it was to learn every-thing about a horse farm, Sunnie knew she was up to the task at hand. There were times when Alvin and Nellie had to bring her back down to earth, but all in all they were happy for her. Sometimes Morgan had to insist Sunnie stay at home or invite Kim and Kelly to the 'Willow Farm'.

Trusting relationships were being built as this young teenage girl continued her education in the horse business. There was something special she loved in each person at the 'Willow Farm'. Emilio was patient, taught Sunnie Spanish and how to care for each creature. Cole taught her much about the Thoroughbred and Walker breeds. It would be a few years before he taught her about the financial end.

The first few times Sunnie mounted a horse, she fell off. Cole was trying to boost her up, but she rolled headfirst right off the other side. This brought about group laughter from Ms. Morgan, Emilio and Cole. Morgan tried to contain herself, but replied, "Great job Sunnie. How does the belly of that horse look to you?" Then Morgan held her hand over her mouth and let out a giggle.

"I'll never get this. It's hopeless," Sunnie said, morti-fied, as she walked around to the left side of the horse again. As she looked up at Cole, he had his head tilted back and was laughing so hard he could barely catch his breath. At this point, Sunnie wasn't sure she would ever get on that horse. The embarrassment was too much.

The traumatized look on Sunnie's face finally caught Morgan's attention, so she quickly explained, "I'm laughing, my dear, because it reminds me of the first few times I tried to ride. Believe me, it will come. Before you know it, you will be a great equestrian."

Cole also tried to ease Sunnie's awkward moment. After all, he didn't do so well his first few mounts either. "Girl, this is sooo funny to us because we all have been there. You don't start off being an expert rider," he reassured Sunnie.

Sunnie still was not convinced that she would ever be able to learn how to ride a horse. But within a week, she finally managed to stay in the saddle, and within a few months, she had learned a great deal about the proper way to ride a horse. As time passed, with Morgan's careful grooming, Sunnie was also learning how to be a lady as well. She was quite proud of herself.

Weeks and, even months, passed. Before Sunnie realized it, her fourteenth birthday was only a month away. It was also almost time for the Kentucky Derby. Morgan had talked with Alvin and Nellie about Sunnie's grades and taking her to Churchill Downs. Sunnie had kept her promise. She was on the honor roll. Her parents agreed that it would be a good experience. Since Sunnie was learning about thoroughbreds, she might as well see them in all their glory.

Ah, the famous Kentucky Derby! The most exciting two minutes in sports. The Derby festivities started in Louisville two weeks prior with the world's largest fireworks and air show down by the Ohio River. Numerous other events led up to Derby day: boat races, marathons, bed races, the balloon glow, balloon races and many more. These things all helped put Kentucky on the map.

Racing was often seen as a sport for the rich, for only they can afford these beautiful creatures. However, it really was a sport for those who love horses and wagers. After all, it was what Kentucky was known for. Churchill Downs in Louisville was old and nostalgic, but refurbished. The Keeneland racetrack in Lexington was smaller, but many horse farms flanked it, including the track itself. What a beautiful sight!

When that first Saturday in May arrived, Oliver, Ms. Morgan, and Cole picked up Sunnie around ten AM. It would be over an hour's ride to the track. For the occasion, Momma had bought Sunnie a new pale yellow sundress with small white daisies at the base of each strap. Her white straw hat had a yellow band that supported small daisies on the right. Sunnie's shoes were white sandals. Nellie always kept some petty cash around for unexpected necessities. She kept it hidden in a coffee can way back in the cabinet under the sink. So she used some of this cash to help dress Sunnie for the occasion.

Morgan was adorned in a black dress with white trim around the neckline, sleeves and hem. Upon her white, wide-brim hat was a wide, black band that supported a small red rose. Morgan's shoes and clutch purse were black. Miss Sunshine thought Ms. Morgan was so beautiful and elegant that day. There was no way her attire was purchased at the local mercantile. Sunnie was not at all familiar with designer clothing, but she knew Ms. Morgan's attire had to have been purchased at a fancy store.

At the Downs, Oliver drove up to the gate through the traffic congestion and let them all out. As Cole exited the car, Sunnie tried not to stare at him. This was the first time she had seen him in a suit and tie. Cole's suit was light tan and his shirt a medium-blue. His tie consisted of shades of tans, yellows and blues. She thought he was very handsome.

They went up several floors to something called Millionaire's Row. Sunnie knew from watching TV what that meant. Ms. Morgan and Cole introduced Sunnie to all of their business acquaintances and friends, even the mayor and a few famous people. Everyone was dressed to the hilt. There was a lot of cheering and plenty to eat and drink. For each race, Sunnie picked out the horse's name that she liked best and cheered it on. Surprisingly, most of them won. Morgan and Cole were not in the habit of making wagers and did not encourage it.

"Well, Sunnie, you seem to have a knack for picking the winners," Cole bragged, with twinkling, amused eyes.

"You think so?" She was proud of herself, and once again pleased by Cole's affirmations.

"Yes ma'am," Cole said reassuring her with a radiant smile.

Sunnie felt her face turning red, so she turned her head and began speaking to Morgan. "Ms Morgan, this is one of the most exciting days I've ever had. We've always watched the Derby on TV, but this is much better in person."

"Your parents told me you were on the honor roll at school. I'm very proud of you, Sunnie," Ms. Morgan praised, giving her young protégée a warm glance. "To reward you, I thought you would like to see these lovely creatures do what they are trained to do. We don't often get to see them after they leave the farm. So I gather you are enjoying yourself?"

"Yes ma'am!" Sunnie exclaimed, nodding her head. "And I've enjoyed meeting some very important people too."

"Sunnie, don't let all this glitter get to you," Morgan took a second to lecture with a trace of concern in her eyes. "These people are just like you and me. They all enjoy racing, but have their own jobs to do. Remember everyone, including *you*....," she said lightly touching the girl's shoulder, "is special in their own way."

"I know, but you are used to this. I haven't been away from the farm or Pleasureville much."

"You will get used to this in time," Morgan said with a knowing grin.

"You know, Pat Day is my favorite jockey. I always cheer him on."

"He is riding in the next race," Morgan told Sunnie, pointing to her racing program. "Come, we will go to the paddock to meet him. He is riding our client's horse."

"Meet Pat Day! You're kidding?" Pat Day was a prominent jockey, one of the best in his field. He had won a lot of races and was very much in demand. Sunnie was beside herself with excitement over the prospect of actually getting to meet this great horseman.

"Cole, please escort us to the paddock, and take Sunnie's picture with Pat Day and the horse he is riding, Run Baby Run."

"Mrs. Willow, I would be glad to," Cole told her, making a hook out of his right arm. Sunnie eagerly linked her arm through his, and Morgan flanked his other side. Sunnie's crush led her down a brief dream world where she imagined herself as Cole's date. Cole began leading the ladies to the elevators that would land near the paddock where they would encounter the jockey. He enthusiastically told his young student as he turned and looked her in the eyes, "Sunnie, Pat's horse is going to win the next race. I'm sure of it. You should root for Run Baby Run," Cole instructed.

Sunnie nodded her head. "I surely will. There's no way this horse can lose."

When they finally arrived at the paddock, Sunnie saw that her favorite jockey knew Ms. Morgan and Cole. After all, he had ridden many horses that came from the 'Willow Farm'. As Pat approached Morgan and Cole with a smile, he shook both their hands.

"Pat, it is so good to see you. You are doing very well today." Morgan knew, even better than Mr. Day, what his daily stats were. Although this man was a jockey, he was not a man who made wagers. Those who knew him well were very aware of this. Pat was more interested in bringing people to know Jesus.

"Morgan, Cole, it is great to see you both. This is a fine horse I'm riding in this race. Of course, you know that," Pat reaffirmed. He then looked straight at Sunnie.

Morgan turned to Sunnie and placed her arm around the girl's shoulders. "This is Sunnie, our new apprentice, who we hope to teach every aspect of our business."

Pat reached for Sunnie's hand and shook it as he said, "It is good to meet you, Sunnie. I've been to 'Willow Farm'. If you want to learn about horses, that farm is the best place to be.

Sunnie was so in awe of this famous jockey that she could barely bring herself to speak back to him. "Mr. Day, you are my very favorite jockey. I always root for you on Derby day. I can't believe I'm really meeting you."

"Well young lady, you really are. Cole, I see you have a camera. Sunnie come over here with me beside Run Baby Run. Let's get a picture for your photo album. When you get it developed, I'll try to autograph it." Sunnie was so pleased to find that Pat Day was a very humble and gracious man. Cole stepped forward and took about three pictures to make sure there would be at least one good one.

"Mr. Day, you have just made my day," Sunnie said as she turned away from the horse and gave Pat a big hug. If this wasn't the icing on the cake for Sunnie, nothing else would be. Could any moment in time get any better than this experience?

This action put a big smile on the jockey's face. "Please excuse me. I need to get instructions from this horse's trainer. I hope to see you soon." It was time for the jockey to get on with the work at hand.

"We need to get back to our seats before this next race," Morgan instructed.

Again, Cole offered his arm to Sunnie as an escort, and again, she quickly took it. Although Sunnie had been rooting on Pat Day with every race he ran, this seemed to be the most important one of all. The whole chain of events that had just transpired gave Sunnie a type of out-of-body experience. In other words, it was too good to be true.

The members of the 'Willow Farm' went back to Millionaire's Row and went to the outside seating area. "And their off," the announcer shouted. As the race started, Pat was close to the rear. But as they rounded the first turn, he was beginning to make his way towards the front. Sunnie was jumping and shouting as she pounded the railing with her hands. Slowly, but surely the jockey aboard Run Baby Run came down the straight away.

The announcer shouted, "Run Baby Run has just won the race by a head's length."

Sunnie was beside herself at this point. She could hardly catch her breath. Morgan and Cole looked at each other and just grinned. It was sooo refreshing to see excitement for something that seemed so commonplace to them. Sunnie brought out a new way for them to enjoy these horses.

Cole had discussed his favorite horse with Sunnie for the actual running of the Derby. Of course, Sunnie had to cheer on the same horse. Her schoolgirl crush was kicking in further.

The day passed ever so quickly, and it was time to go home. Ms. Morgan had been invited to several Derby parties, but rarely attended. Even though she was a very wealthy and influential woman, she wished to keep grounded and stay at the farm with her extended family. Her love for Sunnie was growing, as was Cole's. They both enjoyed seeing her face as she experienced everything. They were so used to the horses and events that surrounded them. It was refreshing to see the newness and joy through Sunnie.

The excitement of the day exhausted Sunnie, so in the car on the drive home, she leaned her head upon Cole's shoulder and fell fast asleep. Cole and Morgan couldn't help but smile.

At the Bader farm, when Oliver opened the car door, Sunnie awoke and smiled. Her day wasn't a dream. It really had happened. Sunnie stepped out of the Rolls and turned back toward the car. "I really enjoyed myself. Thanks so much for taking me today," she told both Morgan and Cole with the most glorious of smiles on her face.

"The pleasure was all ours," Morgan returned. Cole nodded his agreement.

Alvin and Nellie had been to the Garrett's to watch the races. Being a Kentuckian, how could you not celebrate Derby day? Alvin and Nellie greeted Sunnie at the door and waved goodbye to the car load of people. "How was your day, young lady?" Alvin asked, placing his arm around his daughter and leading her into the house.

"It was exciting, and I learned a lot. I even got to meet Pat Day and have my picture taken with him and the horse he road. He won the race, Daddy! Now, where are the boys? I want to say hi to them before I take a bath and go to bed. I'm really tired, and chores come early before church." Sunnie wasn't going to boast about her day unless they asked. She was learning that the things they enjoyed were important too, and running her mouth was getting tiresome to them.

"They're upstairs in David's room working on a puzzle," Nellie said. As Sunnie broke away from her father's embrace and made her way toward the stairs, Nellie glanced at Alvin and whispered, "Perhaps she's finally learned that all that braggin' is not ladylike."

"You may be right, Nellie. I know she's overwhelmed, but the boys and her friends have to be tired of listenin' to her. I think Morgan has taught Sunnie a lot about bein' a lady. She is a good influence on our Sunnie. My little girl is growin' up. It's so hard to watch, and yet it's great to see her develop into the person she's becomin'," he said, sounding wistful. Then he added with a happy twinkle in his eyes, "We've got great kids, Nellie. My proud buttons are just poppin' off."

"Mine are too. We've got a great life and a great family. God has been very good to us," she said, draping an arm around Alvin's back and laying her head on his shoulder. After a few moments, a thought occurred to her. Raising her head and looking Alvin in the eye, Nellie suggested, "Maybe we should have Morgan and Cole to dinner. I wonder if Morgan would care if we invite Emilio too. Sunnie thinks a lot of him, and he's taught her a lot of Spanish."

"Nellie, I think that sounds like a fine idea," Alvin agreed. He gave his bride a warm, approving kiss on the forehead. Then he suggested, "Why don't we go watch a little TV and unwind for the day?"

"Sounds good, Alvin," Nellie agreed, and they made there way into the living room to relax and enjoy being together for the evening.

On Monday morning, Nellie called Morgan to invite her and her two top hands to dinner on Friday. Of course, Morgan graciously accepted. She thought it was important for Cole and Emilio to see the wonderful old house and tree farm.

When they arrived at six-thirty PM, the aroma coming from the kitchen was heavenly. Nellie was a good cook thanks to her mother Emma. She had prepared a large pot roast with carrots, mashed potatoes and gravy, asparagus, salad, homemade rolls, and apple cobbler with iced tea and coffee. Sunnie had set the dining room table with Emma's antique china and silverware.

Nellie walked out of the kitchen as her guests entered the foyer. "Welcome neighbors."

"Something sure smells good, Mrs. Bader. I love home cooking," Cole complimented, rubbing his stomach.

"Yes, Nellie, it does smell divine," Morgan agreed.

"Señor and Señora Bader, buenas noches. Gracias a la inclusión de me."

At this point Sunnie glanced at Daddy and the boys. They were now getting a taste of some of her Spanish lessons.

Nellie replied thank you hoping it was the correct response. "Cole, Emilio, please call us Alvin and Nellie. Dear, would you please seat everyone in the dinin' room? Sunnie, will you help me serve?"

After everyone was seated, Alvin said a wonderful grace. There was plenty of conversation and laughter. Cole talked a great deal with David, Ethan and Jonas. He was very interested in learning about trains and Uncle Bobby's model town. At times, Sunnie would just study everyone enjoying themselves and grin. She liked how well Cole got along with her family, and daydreamed of what it might be like for him to be a part of her family. The thought made her smile.

After desert and coffee, Nellie instructed Alvin to take the guests into the parlor while she and Sunnie cleared the table.

"Please let me assist you, Nellie," Morgan insisted as they all vacated their chairs at the dining room table. "I know you must have worked hard to put on such a delicious meal."

"Oh, I wouldn't hear of it, Morgan. You have servants that do this work for you."

"Nellie, I insist. After all, I have only recently had servants. I know what it takes to cook a meal and clean up. Besides, I'll enjoy us girls having some one-on-one."

"Okay then," Nellie begrudgingly agreed. They all grabbed some dirty dishes from the table and headed to the kitchen.

The girls talked about baking for the church bazaar and how Mr. Perkins was supplying Morgan now with her favorite teas. There was also some talk about how good Pastor Noah's sermons were. After the table was cleared, the dishes and pots were washed with Morgan drying them and placing the pieces on the table. Nellie still felt a little strange having Morgan help with the dishes. "Let's join everyone in the parlor," she said.

Cole and Emilio seemed very interested in how the family grew their food and supplied the furniture store with wood. "I hear the capital always gets its Christmas tree from you. If it is as beautiful as the one Ms. Morgan had this past year, it probably was something else," Cole praised. Although Cole loved the horse business, he was intrigued by Alvin's method of tree farming. Looking around, he commented, "I love this house. It reminds me of my childhood on our farm. I like what you have done to it. I would be proud to have something like this, especially if my parents passed it down to me." Cole had been around horses all his life, but his childhood farm was nothing compared to the Bader's or the 'Willow Farm'. It was shortly after his parent's passing that he went to work for Mrs. Willow.

"I agree, señor," Emilio chimed in. "My family is poor and living in Me-i-co. I try to send them money whenever I can. I was lucky enough to get work at the racetrack. There I learned mucho acerca de los caballos. Señor, I mean to say much about horses."

Alvin grinned, "Thanks for the Spanish lesson."

"Mr. Emilio, Sunnie is teaching us the Spanish she learns from you. We've never been out of the country and never out of Kentucky," David said.

"I am mucho contento to help Sunnie. She is a good student."

"I believe that means 'much glad'." Ethan was trying to show off what he had learned.

"It means 'much happy'. When speaking Spanish, sometimes our verbs are at the end of sentences, and we add gender to objects." The kids enjoyed listening to Emilio. His accent was like music to their ears.

When the girls joined the group in the parlor, Nellie blurted, "Well, have you men solved all the world's problems?"

Cole spoke up as he tapped his cheek with his forefinger, "Of course, now if we could just implement our plans," he laughed.

Alvin was impressed with Cole and Emilio. They seemed to be the finest of gentlemen. As these three farmers from very different worlds chatted, they were becoming good friends as they learned from each other. It was also apparent the respect they shared for one another. Nellie's dinner invite for Morgan, Cole and Emilio had turned out to be a very wise idea.

Chapter 15

It was mid-summer and Sunnie's birthday was approaching. Morgan had called and asked if she could personally speak with Alvin and Nellie, preferably without the children around. It was agreed, and the kids were sent to the Garretts to visit.

"What do you think this is all about, Alvin? Morgan was pretty serious over the phone," Nellie pointed out. Her eyes had a tinge of worry in them.

"If I had to guess, I would say it's about Sunnie's birthday, but that is just a guess. If I'm right though, I'm concerned that it may be something extravagant," Alvin shared, sounding a bit concerned himself.

Morgan arrived in the usual manner, in her Rolls. She was wearing her work clothes consisting of dark blue jeans and a white T-shirt with the 'Willow Farm' logo on the back. Her leather boots were black tie-ups. Although she was still elegant and immaculate, there was a scent of leather and horses about her. "Thank you for seeing me," she said as she entered the front door. Sunnie's parents escorted her into the parlor. I have a special gift in mind for Sunnie's birthday, but I wouldn't think of giving it to her without your permission."

Alvin looked at Nellie as if to say, "I surmised right."

"As you know, I have been teaching Sunnie to ride. She has become a good intermediate rider."

"Yes, we know she's been gettin' lessons." Alvin looked at Nellie again with raised eyebrows.

"I can see by your expression that what I'm about to purpose may not sit well with either of you, but please hear me out. Sunnie is such an all-around good student, both at school and at my horse farm. She studies and works diligently. Because Sunnie is becoming a great asset to me, I would like to give her a Tennessee Walking colt to call her own. She already cares for it. We have a gentleman that can give them dressage training. Please let me give you an explanation. Dressage means 'training' in French. It is occasionally referred to as 'Horse Ballet' which is smooth response to a skilled rider's minimal aids. The purpose is to develop, through standardized progressive training methods, a horse's natural athletic ability and willingness to perform. They also have dressage competitions in the summer Olympics." Morgan was an accomplished rider herself in the equestrian dressage.

"Yes, we've watched the competitions on TV. Morgan, I know how well Sunnie is doin' and havin' a horse all her own is a dream of hers. But ...." Alvin said, pausing and looking down at the floor. When he looked back up at Morgan, he truthfully stated, "We could never come close to letting her have somethin' of this stature. I'm also concerned about the boys and how this would make them feel." Morgan's generous proposal was unsettling to Alvin, and he wanted to make his feelings known.

"Nellie, Alvin, we have become good friends," Morgan said, looking from Nellie to Alvin. "I would never do anything to undermine you or hurt the boys. This horse will be kept exclusively at my farm. If you wish, the boys need not know about it. I don't think that anything you give Sunnie for her birthday would mean any less to her because of this. Since I have known this child, she has told me so many times of her love for you and her brothers. She is proud to be a part of this family. If I were you, I would not underestimate her."

"Even if we agreed, there is no way Sunnie could keep her 'dream come true' a secret from her brothers or friends.

I'm not sure how to handle this," Alvin stated, scratching his chin.

Suddenly Morgan had an idea. "Sunnie has been working all this time. We know she is too young to work for pay, but the boys do not. What if we explained to them that this was her pay? Nellie, what do you think?" she asked, looking her square in the eye.

"Morgan, I still have reservations about this, but there is a part of me that wouldn't want to keep Sunnie from havin' her dream. Although your plan seems sensible, I just don't want anyone hurt. We couldn't ever equal this gift. Alvin, I just don't know what we should do," she said, sounding extremely torn. Her troubled eyes were locked with Alvin's, pleading for him to provide a feasible solution.

"Well we've always taught the kids that it's not the cost of the gift, but the thought that counts. This definitely would put *that* lesson to the test," Alvin stated, tapping his fingers on his legs.

"I will not do this without your approval. Maybe you both could discuss my idea and get back to me," Morgan said.

"Yes, I think that would be best," Alvin agreed, nodding his head. Alvin was the head of the house, but he and his bride made family decisions together. "Thanks for talkin' to us first, Morgan."

"I would never do this without talking to you both first," Morgan assured Alvin as she stood. "I should be on my way. I look forward to hearing from you," she told them. Morgan approached Alvin then and shook his hand. Turning, she found that Nellie had also risen to her feet. She enfolded her into a warm embrace. Morgan wanted to reassure both Alvin and Nellie that no matter what, they were friends.

As Morgan reached the front door, she turned and said, "You know, I've just had a couple more ideas. The colt could be a gift from all of us."

"That's still not fair to the boys. They are also our treasures from heaven," Nellie stated, shaking her head.

"That brings me to my second thought. On Sunnie's birthday, we could also give the boys an early birthday gift. I know they love trains. I could have Oliver drive you to the train station in Noblesville, Indiana where they offer several train rides, or perhaps a puppy would be appropriate. My friend has Golden Retriever puppies. I know you wish only to have the animals you can eat, but perhaps you can make an exception. Nevertheless, please carefully think over these ideas. However you want to handle this is fine with me."

"We will get back to you within the week," Alvin assured her again.

Morgan could be very persuasive if need be, but the last thing she wished to do was create a strain between her and the Baders. They were colleagues in a sense but with different production lines.

"Very well," Morgan agreed. Opening the front door, she headed toward her car.

When Oliver had driven Morgan away, Nellie looked up at Alvin with sad eyes. "How can we compete with this? I want Sunnie to have every opportunity she can. I want her dreams to come true, yet I don't want her to get spoiled. I just don't know what we should do."

"I know how you feel. We need to think about all the options and weigh them carefully," Alvin said, sinking his hands into the pockets of his jeans.

"It will be on my mind until we've made a decision," Nellie told him.

"Together we'll decide what's right," Alvin assured her, draping a reassuring arm around his bride and leading her away from the door.

Each night that week when Nellie and Alvin went to bed, they discussed Morgan's proposals. Finally a decision was made.

A week later, Momma and Daddy informed the children that they needed to run an errand for Sunnie's birthday. So they left in the old truck to visit Morgan.

Sunnie thought, "I wonder what they have up their sleeves. Something is *definitely* up with that," she said as she tapped her cheek and looked up. Sunnie just knew it was something very special. She caught Momma and Daddy whispering and grinning a lot. She questioned the boys, but they had no idea what their parents had concocted. Sunnie loved her birthdays. Her parents always made the children feel special, kind of like they were blessed each year with a new birth all over again.

Ethan said, "It's probably a bundle of switches or a bucket of coal. Yeah, that's it."

"You're thinking of Santa and Christmas," she reminded him.

"Oh, I must have gotten confused," he laughed jokingly. That Ethan was a real kidder.

Sometimes being outnumbered by these boys was a challenge for Sunnie. She thought of herself as a mother hen to them, but, oh, how she loved each one.

When the Baders arrived at the 'Willow Farm', Theo directed them to the 'Bluegrass' barn where Morgan and Cole awaited them in the office.

"It is good to see you both," Cole greeted. "Please sit down."

As Alvin and Nellie settled into two chairs on the other side of the desk, Alvin cut right to the chase, "Morgan, this was a very difficult decision for us. We talked about it every night."

"Before you say anything else, Alvin, not only have we become good neighbors and friends; but I feel you are my extended family," Morgan told them with her eyes growing a little misty.

"Well the feelin' is mutual," Alvin agreed while petting Nellie's hand. The friendship between these two families had indeed blossomed. Morgan's wealth had not ever entered into it until now. Alvin smiled and told her, "Nellie and I have agreed that Sunnie can have the horse. But….if it's okay with you, Morgan, we would like to say the colt is from you and us. We also think the boys would like the train ride even though they've always wanted a dog. That should be from all of us too, but Morgan, you must realize we can't compete with someone of your stature. We just can't have this happenin' every birthday or Christmas." Nervously, Alvin fidgeted in his chair.

"Alvin, you and Nellie are wonderful parents," Morgan praised, returning his smile. She was secretly thrilled by their decision. "I assure you that I will keep my gifts low-key and always with your approval. If you can arrive here on Sunnie's birthday after church, we can give the children their gifts."

Cole chimed in, "Emilio and I would like to give *all* your boys the Golden Retriever, but only if you are okay with it."

Nellie and Alvin looked at each other, and Nellie nodded yes. "Sure, but please remember not to upscale each year. We really don't want to handle another situation like this."

"Then it is agreed. Thank you for helping me make this dream come true for your lovely daughter," Morgan said with her face now glowing with happiness.

"Perhaps you, Cole and Emilio can come to Sunnie's birthday dinner. I know the kids will be grateful," Nellie invited.

"Invitation accepted," Morgan said, pushing back her desk chair and rising to her feet. "I hate to rush off, but I must make an important long-distance call to a client. I look forward to seeing you and the children on Sunday."

"See you then," Alvin said as he and Nellie stood and started away from the office. They were all very happy with the decision they had made and looked forward to Sunnie's birthday.

That birthday morning, Nellie fixed Sunnie's favorite breakfast. Church service was as usual. Morgan always sat with the Baders.

Pastor Noah was standing on the stoop after the service. "Awe, I hear someone turned fourteen today. Now who might that be?"

"Pastor, you know it's me," Sunnie said with a giggle, pointing at herself.

"Well, happy birthday, Sunnie," he gushed, reaching to lightly touch her hand.

"Thank you, Pastor," she replied with a toothy grin. Then Sunnie rushed off to the car with her parents. She could hardly wait to get home.

On the drive home, the Baders made a stop for gas to stall a bit. Instead of going straight, Daddy turned into the 'Willow Farm'. "Why are we going here, Daddy?" Sunnie asked, confused and curious.

"Well my daughter, we had to hide your gift here so you wouldn't find it," Alvin told her, looking at Sunnie in the rearview mirror. There was a conniving twinkle in his eyes.

"How clever, but it *sure* must be big. Momma's good at hiding gifts," Sunnie said with a confused look on her face.

"We'll need to walk around the back of the house and stand by the backyard gate," Alvin told her as he parked the car in front of Morgan's house.

Morgan had managed to quickly change and make her way to the 'Kentucky' barn before they arrived. When she caught sight of the Baders as they approached, she shouted from the barn doors, "Sunnie, you must close your eyes and do not peek."

As Sunnie stopped and squeezed her eyes shut to oblige Morgan, she heard a light clip-clop coming her way. She thought to herself, why would Morgan bring a horse from the barn since this wasn't a day of work for her? Sunnie's parents were looking at their sons with gestures for them to keep quiet. The boys did all they could do to not make any sounds.

Alvin was standing behind Sunnie with his hands placed upon her shoulders. Nellie was standing beside him holding Sunnie's hand. "Open you eyes, birthday girl," Alvin said, squeezing her shoulders.

Sunnie's eyes flew open to find a horse named Sophia standing in front of her. "Why did you bring Sophia to me? Must I groom her on my birthday?" she asked, sounding a bit disappointed now. A slight frown had replaced her usual smile.

"Sunnie, Sophia is yours to keep," Nellie explained, placing her arm around her daughter's waist and giving her a squeeze. "She's a gift from Morgan, Daddy and me."

"My....my own horse!" Sunnie stuttered, her eyes wide with disbelief. "You're letting me have my own horse, Daddy!?" she asked, studying Daddy's face carefully. She held her breath while she waited for his reply. Daddy had always been so adamant about having only animals they could eat that Sunnie was finding it hard to believe that he would concede to her having beautiful Sophia now.

"Yes Sunnie, I am," Alvin confirmed. But he quickly added, "as long as you keep it here at the 'Willow Farm'."

"Yes sir, I will!" Sunnie promised. Then she looked at Morgan to confirm, "That is if it is okay with you, Ms. Morgan?"

"Yes Sunnie. Of course it is," Morgan agreed. Once more, she was very pleased by the joy she saw on this special young girl's face. Sunnie was fourteen and becoming a very well groomed young lady, partly in thanks to Morgan.

"Wow, Miss Ladybug! Now you can ride off into the sunset," David shouted.

Sunnie barely heard him, because she was busy giving out hugs and kisses to her parents and Morgan. She simply couldn't believe her Daddy gave in, but she also knew Ms. Morgan could be *very* persuasive.

When Sunnie finished bestowing her thanks to everyone, she went over to Sophia and touched her face to the side of the horse's head, gently stroking her mane. "You're mine now, Sophia," she told the colt. "I'll take great care of you," she promised as she tried to blink back grateful tears. The water works came down Sunnie's cheeks in full force anyway. She was so in awe of what just transpired that she began to bawl.

Alvin knew it was his place to calm his girl down. After all, it was he who was adamant about not having a horse. He looked at the women, winked and nodded. Alvin walked to Sunnie, wrapped his arms around his only daughter, rubbed her back and said, "Girl, this is supposed to be a happy time. Let's see that big smile we are so used to seein'."

Sunnie knew Daddy was right. When she wiped her eyes and looked up at her brothers, they were gently waving to her as if to say, "It's OK. Be happy."

Morgan was very touched by Sunnie's love for Sophia. To keep from getting emotional, she quickly turned her attention to Sunnie's brothers. After all, she, Nellie and Alvin had a surprise for them as well.

"Now boys, I know your birthdays are close together this fall. Your parents and I went together and wanted to give you part of your gifts now and the rest later around your birthdays." Morgan pulled an envelope out of her pocket and gave it to David.

Ethan and Jonas gathered on each side as he pulled out what seemed to be tickets. "I don't get it. What is this?" David asked with a puzzled expression on his face.

"Somewhere around your birthdays, you and your parents are taking a long train ride through Indiana."

"A train ride…. a real train ride!?" Jonas exclaimed, clapping his hands with a huge smile on his face.

"Indeed, a real train ride," Morgan assured him, laughing at his enthusiasm.

"Yeh!" the boys all shouted in unison. Now it was David, Ethan and Jonas' turn to go around giving thanks and hugs.

Cole and Emilio emerged from the barn carrying a large box. "Hey, what is all this commotion? Emilio, don't you think these kids are acting a bit silly?"

"Sí, señor Cole. Ellos están siendo muy tonto."

"Sunnie, what did Emilio just say?" Alvin asked.

"Yes, Mr. Cole. They are being very silly."

"Emilio and I have a birthday gift for all you boys. Here in this box," he told them, tapping the side of the container. "Let me set it down. It's very heavy."

As all four gathered around the box, Sunnie said, "Ethan, you open it." As he did, the cutest blonde puppy popped up. It was a Golden Retriever.

"This dog is ours to keep at our house?" Ethan asked, his eyes lighting up with wonder as he reached to pet the pooch.

Nellie said, "Yes, she comes home with us, but the first time you don't care for her or take her out, she will be returned. Understood?" Seeing the delight and awe on all her children's faces, Nellie was now sure that they had made the right decision with all the gifts

"This is the best birthday ever!" Sunnie exclaimed with sparkling eyes. "We promise to take good care of our new pets, don't we boys?" she asked her brothers.

"Yes, we promise," they added one at a time.

Nellie spoke up, "I really must go home and start preparing Sunnie's birthday dinner. We will see you all later around six-thirty."

Sunnie was glad that her other family would be joining them. It would give her and her brothers another opportunity to say thanks. Sunnie and the boys thanked Ms. Morgan, Cole and Emilio one last time for their generosity. As Sunnie headed out towards the car with her parents and brothers, she flashed Cole one last smitten smile. *"He's such a good guy"*, she thought. Her heart was filled with affection.

David was elected to carry the dog since the box was heavy. Sunnie pushed herself between her other two brothers as they walked towards the car. "Guys, this is the greatest birthday of all!" she cooed, placing her arms around her youngest brothers.

"Yeah, the very best," Ethan agreed. David and Jonas enthusiastically nodded their agreement. Wide smiles graced all their faces. They were all ecstatic about their gifts.

All the way home the puppy licked and nipped at David's chin. Jonas and Ethan eagerly sat on each side so they could pet the pup. Puppies being puppies, it was hard to hold her in the box. Of course she had a little accident in the box. What's a puppy to do?

That evening when the guests arrived, they came bearing more gifts. "The rest of our crew chipped in and sent over this cage, some food, and puppy toys." Cole didn't even have to ask. The farmhands were more than happy to do it.

Holding the new family member, Ethan walked up to the guests. "Ah, there's the little girl," Cole said as he petted her head. "Have you guys given this little doll a name?"

"We have some names picked out: Sandy, Frisky, Dolly, or maybe Cuddles." Ethan thought he was the project manager of naming the new puppy.

Cole had a suggestion. "What if you named her Biscuit? She is kind of the color of your mom's delicious biscuits."

"I like that name best," Jonas chimed in.

"What do you guys think?" David really wanted the puppy to have a name.

The boys gathered in a huddle and talked amongst themselves while the grownups chatted in the foyer. They were getting a kick out of seeing the children gather privately for this big discussion.

When they separated, Jonas announced with serious eyes, "We want to call her Biscuit."

Not only was Cole thrilled about giving the kids a dog, he was happy they liked the name he suggested. "I have one more suggestion," he told them, holding up one finger. "If you keep her in the cage until you play with her or take her outside, she will be easier to potty train. A dog usually won't dirty its cage. Just take her outside each time you get her out. Give her a one-word command....'potty'. Remember puppies like to chew. Keep anything you treasure out of reach. You guys will get the hang of it. I have trained several dogs. If you have any questions, just call me."

Nellie and Alvin still had concerns about having a pet to raise. Raising a puppy wouldn't be quite as easy as the boys thought. Sunnie, on the other hand, knew that taking care of animals was serious business. She appreciated Cole taking the time to instruct them on how to care for the dog. He was so intelligent about everything. She thought Cole was just the finest man, other than Daddy, that she had ever known. As Cole looked over at Sunnie and smiled, she felt her stomach flutter. She glanced down at her feet and rushed off to the kitchen to help Momma with the food.

Supper was grand. Nellie had made spaghetti sauce and meatballs from scratch. There was plenty of salad and garlic bread. She baked a sheet cake with a horse head atop it. Her cake decorating impressed Morgan.

"Nellie, have you thought about baking cakes for a living?" Morgan suggested.

"Not really. I do bake for the church bazaar, but my specialty is quilts. I usually make one or two quilts a year and sell them."

"You hand-make quilts?" Morgan asked, impressing anew. "I must have one. I would treasure it always. Perhaps after dinner, I can pick out a pattern."

"Sure. I will be startin' my next one when the kids go back to school," Nellie told her. Nellie would be more than happy to make Morgan a quilt. She was very grateful to this woman for all she had done for her children.

After supper, Nellie took Morgan upstairs and showed her the quilts in each bedroom. Morgan selected the style and colors that would best accent her master bedroom.

These families were blending well. Relationships were growing. What a lovely time to be in Kentucky.

Chapter 16

Sunnie was growing up right before everyone's eyes. Every day for her was a new adventure. At times, it was hard for her to balance all her activities, but she was determined not to let anyone down. Sunnie was not a typical teenager. She didn't have a rebellious bone in her body. She never wanted to disappoint those she cared about.

In the winter, school and family still came first. If this freshman's grades were not up to par, she would not be allowed to go to the horse farm. At country schools, foreign languages were not offered as elective high school subjects. That's where Emilio came in. Week by week, month by month, Sunnie was speaking more fluent Spanish and trying to pass a little of it onto her family. This pleased Emilio so much. He did not have any children of his own, and this adolescent, whose mind was like a sponge, seemed more like a daughter to him. Emilio had such a soft place in his heart for his student. On the days she was at the farm, somehow, chores didn't feel like work at all. Those days passed ever so quickly.

Summer gave Sunnie more time to be at the 'Willow Farm', but Alvin and Nellie expected her to pull her weight at home at all times. One day in late August, Sunnie reported to Emilio as usual. They were getting a new horse to board. It was important she know how to care for their new client's horse. Sunnie strutted into Emilio's office with confidence.

She walked over to him as he stood from his chair and shook his hand with the usual big smile on her face. "Buenos dias, Emilio. Cómo estás hoy? (Good morning, Emilio. How are you today?)" Sunnie was so proud of her Spanish skills.

Emilio had a smirk on his face. He was up to something, but the apprentice's eagerness didn't permit her to notice. "Buenos dias, Miss Sunnie. Me alegro de que esté finalmente aquí (I'm glad you are finally here). Tenemos mucho trabajo por hacer (We have much work to do). Echemos mirar los instrucción del propietario en el nuevo caballo (Let us look at the owner's instructions on the new horse). Estamos poniendo Tess en el tercer puesto de la granja de Kentucky (We are putting Tess in the third stall of the Kentucky barn)."

Sunnie was flabbergasted. She only understood a little of what Emilio was saying. She had her right arm out toward her Spanish teacher waving her hand. "Geely whiz! Slow down, Emilio. Tell me what you are saying. I want to make sure I care for this new horse properly."

Emilio proceeded to converse with his helper, but in a much slower manor. "Sí señorita (Yes, young lady). I se ralentizaará (I will slow down). El remolque sólo arrancado (The trailer just pulled up). Que nos salen al encuentro de Tess (Let us go out to meet Tess)." This kind and gentle teacher could see that his student did not understand as much as she thought she could.

As Sunnie and Emilio walked from the 'Bluegrass' barn, into and through the 'Kentucky' barn, the frustrated girl asked, "Emilio, are you going to speak Spanish all day?"

"Sí señorita," he said with his head nodding up and down as he patted Sunnie's head. Emilio knew it was for Sunnie's benefit that she learn conversational Spanish, so he added facial expressions and hand gestures. But for the rest of the day, Emilio spoke only Spanish to Sunnie. If it were not for Emilio's inventive sign language, his student would have been very lost as to what he needed her to do.

Emilio's hard lesson pretty much took the sail out of Sunnie for the day. Soon, it was time to go home. Exhausted, she walked slowly through the gate and up to the lanai where Ms. Morgan and Cole were sitting at the table working on the budget.

Morgan heard Sunnie approach. She laid her pen down and turned her head toward Sunnie in order to ask how her day went. "My dear girl, you look exhausted. What ever have you been doing all day?" she questioned, even though she already knew the answer. Emilio had informed his boss of his intentions for the day. Although Morgan felt a little sorry for her friend, she was trying to hold back a smirk.

Sunnie pulled out a chair and literally slouched into it with her arms folded on the table. "Geely whiz! It's Emilio. He wouldn't speak a word of English all day. I was so afraid of missing instructions. It just plain wore me out trying to figure out what he was saying. Please have Oliver take me home," the girl requested as she laid her head upon her arms.

Cole looked up at Mrs. Willow and gave her a wink as he tried to hold back a smile. He reached over to pat Sunnie's hand and tried to console her. "Young lady, there isn't any easy days at this farm. You might as well get used to it. I know you can handle it. You can." He then pulled his hand back and took a drink of iced tea.

Sunnie just looked up at him and stared as if to say, "You've got to be kidding." She was too tired to even notice his touch. She dearly loved Emilio, but wondered if all her lessons from now on would be this hard. After Oliver dropped her off, Alvin and Nellie's daughter slowly strolled into the house where she found Momma in the kitchen.

"How was your day, Dear?" Nellie asked while peeling potatoes. Then she glanced up at Sunnie. What Nellie saw in this glance caused her instant concern. "My word, you look like a whooped puppy," she was quick to comment. Wiping her hands on the kitchen towel, Nellie stopped with her chore and frowned as she asked, "What ever did they have you doin' today?"

"It's Emilio. He didn't speak a word of English all day. His instructions were so confusing. Most of the time, I didn't know what to do," she said, turning her head left to right. Her arms hung limply at her sides. "I worked my brain way too hard. I've got to go to my room and lay down." Sunnie sluggishly walked toward the stairs. Little did she know, Emilio had plans to speak even more Spanish.

"Yes, dear. Supper will be in an hour," Nellie informed her. With a slight frown, Nellie forced a half smile. Life wasn't always easy. She thought Sunnie needed to learn this tough lesson. Supper had to be prepared, so Nellie continued peeling.

Other than Emilio's thought provoking, hands-on, Spanish tutoring from time to time, Sunnie's routine and schedule didn't change much. On both farms, the daily chores had to be done with occasional repairs. The ritual didn't seem to bore her at all. Everything it took to care for the horses was such great pleasure for her, especially caring for her filly, Sophia. Sunnie's horse was bay in color and doing quite well on its dressage training. Some of the movements Sophia and Sunnie were learning were:

Half Halt	Turns using outside reins
Canter	Tempi Change
Pirouetee	Working Trot
Piaffe	Collective Trot
Half-pass	Extended Trot

In spite of all the training, that horse got lots of love from her owner. It was Sunnie's belief that animals should be loved and spoiled. Her brother's dog, Biscuit, was being spoiled too and was equally doing well with her training. Biscuit only had a couple of accidents in the house. She now knew how to sit, lay, and come. Alvin and Nellie were very strict with their sons about the dog. They had better tend to her needs or they would be finding a new home for this beauty.

It was a Saturday in the spring of the next year. Ms. Morgan usually ran Sunnie through her dressage routines early on Saturdays. Sunnie went through the 'Kentucky' barn looking for her teacher, then to the 'Bluegrass' barn where she found Cole sitting behind the desk. She walked over and sat in the first guest chair facing the farm manager.

Cole's boss had given him instructions for Sunnie's day. "Ah, Sunnie I'm glad you are here. I know you are supposed to get a riding lesson today, but Mrs. Willow had to go out of town yesterday. She won't be back until Monday."

The teenager was curious as to what her duties would be for the day. She had a moment's thought that it was nice to have Cole all to herself.

"Well then, what are my duties for the day?" she asked with a slight tilt to her head and her hands palm up?

"I know it won't be exactly like your usual riding lessons, but if you would like, you can ride Sophia along beside me out to the back field to check on a broken fence. You can practice your canters, gallops and such." Cole wanted to salvage her day.

She bent her head down and thought for a second and shook her head 'yes' as she said, "I guess that will work. I haven't seen how all the repairs are done yet. How will we fix it?" Sunnie knew tools would be needed, but her brothers were the ones who helped Daddy fix the fences.

"Once I have assessed the needed repairs, I'll ride back and put the tools into the truck. I may need one of the hands to go back with me. Now, are you up to the ride?" Cole was more than sure Sunnie would say yes. Normally Cole would have taken the truck to the site, but Ms. Morgan had wanted Sunnie to get in a ride today.

"Yes, Cole, I would be glad to ride and observe." There went that pitter-patter in her heart again.

"Go saddle up our horses. I need to talk with José for a few minutes," Cole said as he rose up from the chair and put his hands into his front pockets.

"Yes sir, 'ya, en seguida' (pronto) sir." Although Sunnie was excited about the ride, it was important for her to be as professional and grown-up as possible.

As the two mounted the horses and walked them out into the field, Sunnie's curious mind had questions. "Cole, why haven't you come to church with Ms. Morgan? Everyone there would like to meet you. You would be welcomed."

"Um, that's a good question." Cole paused for a second, then continued. "I guess," he paused again then said, "I guess it is because I went to church so much as a kid. I think I kind of got burned out so to speak. I know that isn't a good excuse, but it's the best explanation I have for now," he said with his face turned towards Sunnie while bouncing on his horse.

The two reached their destination and dismounted. Sunnie didn't want to disturb Cole while he checked things out so she stood by the horses and held onto their reins. She carefully observed his thoroughness. Of course, Cole knew just what to do to fix the fence. "This is a one man job. Let's mount up and head back so I can get this job done today. We don't want to lose any horses."

The couple had put the horses into a trot. Sunnie pulled back on the reins and slowed down to stop behind Cole. With that, he stopped his horse and turned to see why she had fallen behind. He trotted back to see why she stopped, but saw a troubled look on her face. "Is something the matter?" Cole asked as he pulled his horse up beside hers facing the opposite direction.

"Would you do me a favor?" she said with a sheepish look.

Cole had never heard those words come from Sunnie's mouth. She wasn't accustomed to asking favors. "I will try. What is it?"

Sunnie paused for a second. She was a little frightened of what Cole's response would be. She then looked into his eyes and said, "Would you please try to put Jesus back into your heart?" It seemed like minutes, not seconds, before Cole replied.

The farm manager smiled as he looked back into Sunnie's eyes. "Sweetie, He's never left!" Cole knew that church wouldn't save him, only his personal relationship with Christ would. He just didn't talk about it much. Cole thought to himself, "Maybe I do need to start going to church again."

Sunnie smiled back, and then kicked her horse. Off she went into a full gallop as if to indicate she was racing Cole back to the barn, and he was obliging. They were racing as hard as they could. Cole would have won, but he slightly slowed down so Sunnie could reach the barns first. The horses had worked up a good soapy lather. Sunnie removed their tack, hosed them down and put the horses out in the shady pasture.

This day played in Sunnie's mind time and time again. It was important to her that all those she cared dearly about be God fearing people.

In the summer of Sunnie's seventeenth year, Morgan called the Bader home one Friday evening. Alvin and Nellie were in the kitchen drinking coffee and eating a few cookies. Alvin answered the phone.

"Alvin it is so good to hear your voice. How are you and that wonderful family doing?" Morgan said making pleasant conversation.

"Just grand, Morgan," he replied; then inquired, "How about yourself?" Alvin wiped his mouth. Nellie looked up at her man to listen to the conversation. She was wondering what Morgan had up her sleeve.

"We've been very busy lately. The barns are full. We have a lot of training going on. A couple of our farmhands have had a virus. Therefore, we have been also short-handed. You know how farming can be."

"Indeed I do. What's on your mind, Morgan?" Alvin asked, cutting to the chase. He glanced at his bride, and Nellie returned the look. They both knew Morgan was up to something, and she was.

Morgan proceeded, "As you both know, Sunnie has been through a lot of training here at the horse farm, and she is getting some pay now. I felt it is time for us to run her through a series of tests to see if she remembers what she has learned." Morgan knew that Alvin and Nellie were apprehensive about most of her requests. She also knew that it may never be appropriate to tell them of her final plan.

"And....," Alvin said in a condescending tone while waiting for the bomb to fall.

"I know how important it is for Sunnie to pull her weight on your farm, but I was hoping she could stay with me for the weekend. It will take two days to test her skills on riding, caring for the horses, and some of the business at hand. Is it at all possible for you to do without her?" Morgan was not at all sure of what the answer would be.

"Let me ask Nellie. Hold on." Alvin put his hand over the receiver of the phone and quietly told Nellie of Morgan's request. Nellie felt it wasn't worth the hassle to say no, so she nodded yes to Alvin while rolling her eyes and sipping her coffee.

"Okay, Morgan. We'll manage without her. The boys are older now and pull more weight," Alvin said in a reluctant tone.

Morgan had gotten her way again as she knew she would. "Thank you very much. She really needs to go through these challenges. Please tell Sunnie that Oliver will be there tomorrow morning at eight o'clock sharp. It is going to be a busy weekend."

Sunnie was shocked that she was to spend the weekend at the 'Willow Farm'. Her usual week was two or three days, depending on the season.

Morgan had worked very hard with Sunnie on so many things like the proper way to talk, the proper way to be a lady, the proper way to dress, and equestrian dressage training. Most of the leather goods that Sunnie needed for riding were purchased by Morgan. Since these items were kept in the 'Kentucky' tack room, the Baders were not made aware of it. This just helped to keep things calmer between the two families. Ms. Morgan and Cole had shown Sunnie a little about keeping the books for the business, but it was a little confusing not knowing a lot about bookkeeping. That is why the owner of 'Willow Farm' had so many great plans for Sunnie. As Morgan had told the Baders, it was now time to put her apprentice through some testing.

Sunnie found Ms. Morgan sitting at the kitchen table when she arrived for her weekend stay. "Why am I here for the whole weekend?" she asked. Little did Sunnie know, she was going to have a weekend full of those exhausting days.

"Ah, there you are, my dear. Sit for a moment and listen carefully," Morgan said as she patted the chair next to her. Sunnie sat down, but, for a change, didn't say a word.

Morgan continued, "You must know by now how much I care for you." Sunnie started to speak, but Morgan placed her forefinger onto her lips. She wanted to explain her plan completely first. "By the look on your face, I know that you care, very much, for your extended family here." Sunnie shook her head yes. "You have learned a great deal about this farm, how it is run, and the staff. I want to make sure you know most of what's needed to run this farm. For the next two days, I and the staff will be testing you on what you have learned." Sunnie kind of froze, curled up the right side of her lip and looked at Ms. Morgan. "Young lady, you are very capable of handling this. It isn't any different than being tested at school. Just look at it in that manner. Now before you say anything, I need you to know this. I am not getting any younger. Eventually, I will need Cole and you to do more around this farm. Not right now, mind you, but in the future. Now you may speak," Morgan finally permitted.

Sunnie was obsessed with every bit of knowledge she could gain about the horse business. She spoke slowly wanting to tell Ms. Morgan her complete thoughts. "Ms Morgan, I love it here, and I love all the people here. I am especially grateful for the opportunity you have given me. It's been a dream of mine to work with horses. I will be honored for you to test me. It's been a joy to learn. I shouldn't have any problems."

Morgan cupped her hand on Sunnie's cheek. She really was family now. "Then let us get started. Go saddle up Sophia. We will start by putting you through the dressage patterns and movements."

"Yes ma'am," Sunnie agreed with her usual grand enthusiasm. Sunnie then ran out to the barn to prepare. With tears in her eyes, Morgan stood at the lanai doorway and watched her going to the barn. Oh how she needed this girl.

The next two days were unbelievable. While in the corral, Morgan gave Sunnie every dressage command. Emilio quizzed her about everything that she should know on boarding the horses. Cole quizzed her on how clients were handled for breeding their horses. Morgan and Cole asked her many questions about the bookkeeping. They didn't expect her to know everything just yet. The bare necessities were all that was needed for right now. It was a very exhausting weekend for the apprentice.

On Sunday morning, it was church as usual. At the end of the day, Morgan and Cole had Sunnie join them on the lanai. Theo had brought out a pitcher of cold tea and some crumpets. Morgan poured everyone some tea and placed a couple of crumpets on each plate. Boy, did that hit the spot. Looking up at Sunnie she asked, "Well young lady, how do you think you did these past two days?"

"I feel comfortable in saying I did well," Sunnie said with confidence. Then she asked, "Did I?" Sunnie took a sip of tea and bit into a crumpet while looking up at Ms. Morgan, then Cole. She needed to hear the words from the two teachers facing her.

"May I?" Cole asked Mrs. Willow while looking at her. She nodded yes.

"Young lady, you passed everything with flying colors. You should be proud of yourself," Cole stated while touching Sunnie's hand.

With that, she curled up her nose, smiled and sank into the chair. She commenced to continue eating and drinking. From then on, there was a lot of chatter and laughter between the three…. but not so much about business. It was more like friends just having a good time. *Now Mrs. Willow's dreams were coming true.*

Chapter 17

It was the beginning of Sunnie's senior year of high school. A month after graduation, she would be eighteen. Her friends Kim and Kelly were going off to the University of Louisville after high school since their grandparents had left them some money. Sunnie's cousins, Tim and Steve, would also be attending U of L next fall. They both had earned scholarships. Tim was interested in mathematics and Steve wanted to get into financing. Sunnie was happy for her cousins. She always enjoyed these guys because of their dry since of humor. They thoroughly enjoyed teasing Sunnie since she was a good target.

Sunnie wanted to go to college, but knew her parents could not afford it. Daddy did okay with the tree farm. They had savings, but not nearly enough to give four kids a college education.

Cole and Sunnie had become more than friends. Cole and Sunnie's relationship was very strong. Cole was a perfect gentleman and wouldn't think of making any romantic advances toward Sunnie until she was at least eighteen. The age difference was also a concern. Neither of them fooled Ms. Morgan. Unbeknownst to anyone, she had future plans for these two.

By this time, Sunnie had become quite a horse woman. Learning to give her horse undetectable body and leg commands was difficult, but she was mastering it. Sunnie had to take Sophia through many movements and gates such as the halt, salute, and lengthen stride in canter.

She had entered a couple of dressage competitions which were set to music. The dress code for competitors was: white breeches, tall black boots, white shirt with stock tie, dark jacket and cap, derby or top hat. The top hat and dark tailcoat is exclusively for tests above the 4th level.

Morgan was pleased that Sunnie earned third place in her first competition. At Sunnie's next dressage, she came in second place. Sunnie had come so very far and had grown into the finest of ladies.

On this particular Saturday morning, Momma and Sunnie were baking some cookies while the boys were out in the barn helping Daddy with chores.

David, now sixteen, was helping Alvin clean out the stalls. Ethan, fourteen, and Jonas, twelve, were helping by tumbling the bales of hay that way. Tumbling was the best technique and easier on the back than carrying or dragging them.

All of a sudden, Alvin stopped shoveling. David quickly noticed, but thought Daddy was just resting a bit. Daddy was staggering with sweat upon his forehead. Then David realized something wasn't right. "Are you okay, Daddy?"

"I'm not sure. I feel so strange. I'm going out here to sit down a spell." Alvin was out of breath as he spoke and staggered to the barn's center. David was becoming very worried as he followed Alvin out.

Jonas noticed Daddy stumbling and hollered, "Daddy, are you okay?"

At that moment, Alvin grabbed his chest and collapsed to the ground on his back. David called out to him, "Daddy, Daddy, wake up. Please wake up!" But there was no response at all. With that, David's maturity took over. "Guys, stay here with Daddy while I go for help!" David's worst fear was now reality, but he tried to stay hopeful.

Ethan and Jonas knelt on each side of their father. Jonas patted Daddy's hand while Ethan patted his face. Neither got a response. It was very hard for them to wait for that very much needed help.

David ran as fast as he could to the house. He was hoping that Momma and Sunnie were still in the kitchen.

Momma and Sunnie were jolted as the kitchen door was thrown open and David came running into the kitchen shouting, "Come to the barn. Hurry!!! Somethin' is really wrong with Daddy!!! He's lyin'on the ground and not movin'!!!"

Nellie shouted with anxiety, "Sunnie, call Morgan and Cole. Have them come quickly. We may need to take Daddy to the hospital. Now hurry!!!"

As Nellie ran with David to the barn, Sunnie made that call. "Theo, we have an emergency. Something is terribly wrong with Daddy. Please send Ms. Morgan and Cole to our barn."

"I will send them quickly, Sunnie. Please don't worry," Theo assured her.

When Sunnie entered the barn, Daddy still wasn't moving. Nellie kept tapping her husband's face and rubbing his hands. But there was no response. David had a supportive arm around each of his brothers. Ethan and Jonas had red, tear-filled eyes. David just couldn't hold back his tears any longer. He was Daddy's right-hand man. As Sunnie saw the emotion in her brothers, she too began to cry. She walked over and clung to her siblings.

It was only minutes before Morgan and Cole arrived. As they both entered the open area of the barn, Morgan stated while grabbing her chest, "Oh my!! We must get Alvin to the hospital immediately!" This brought back sad memories of her beloved Andrew's death.

Nellie reluctantly separated from Alvin's side as Cole gently touched her shoulder. "Mrs. Willow, can you help Nellie up while I check out Alvin?"

Morgan rushed to her side. "Please dear, come to me. Hold on tight." Morgan had tears flowing down her cheeks as she flung her arms about her good friend. With that, Nellie crunched her arms into herself and laid her head upon Morgan's chest as Morgan gently rubbed Nellie's back. The Bader siblings went to stand by the women.

Cole bent down to check Alvin's jugular vein. Cole's heart sank as he felt nothing. He quickly began to administer CPR and then rechecked for Alvin's pulse a few moments later. He felt sick to his stomach for Nellie, the boys, and especially *his* Sunnie as he still felt *nothing*.

Pulling back from Alvin, Cole stood and turned to face them all. He did not want to utter the words he knew he must, even though the forlorn expression on his face was already telling them a great deal. "I'm afraid Alvin is gone," Cole finally said. His voice sounded far away. "I'm so sorry Nellie," he added with the saddest of eyes.

Nellie gave him an uncomprehending stare. Then as his words settled in, she gave Alvin one last glance and then unexpectedly collapsed to the ground.

"Momma!" Ethan and Jonas shouted and bolted to kneel by her side. With frightened eyes and quivering lips, they looked up at Cole and asked, "She's not dead too, is she!?"

Morgan rushed over and placed a hand on each of the boys' shoulders, "No Ethan and Jonas. Your mother has fainted from shock," she assured them. "She will come around in a few minutes."

Cole said as he looked at the Bader siblings, "We must get your Mother into the house."

While Cole bent and scooped Nellie into his arms and began carrying her from the barn, Sunnie dashed to his side and held onto his arm. Trying to be strong for the women, the boys gathered around Morgan. She held onto David's arm and Ethan's hand as they all walked toward the house.

After Cole had placed Nellie on the sofa in the parlor, he turned and gathered Sunnie into his arms and held her in a tight embrace. There were tears standing in Cole's eyes as well. His heart was breaking because of the pain he knew *his* Sunnie was feeling. He wished he could make it all right for her, but he knew that he could not. He had experienced loosing both parents. There just wasn't any way to make the situation better.

Nellie was coming to. She sat up. Morgan sat down and hugged her. "Are you okay?"

"I dreamed Alvin...," Nellie said fretfully as she looked up at Morgan "It's true!! It's true!!" She uttered with a quivery voice.

As everyone was gathered around Nellie, Morgan tried to comfort her as best she could. She also knew Nellie was too upset to take charge of the situation. "Yes, it's true! Alvin is gone. I'm so very sorry, Nellie. I know how you must feel because I lost my Andrew too. Nellie, it's imperative that we call the county coroner. I will make the call for you. Please don't worry about a thing. I will also make a call to Pastor Noah to let him know what has happened. Is there anything else you need Cole or me to do?"

"No, Morgan. I should be the one making all the calls," she said, seeming rational for a moment. Then she looked away staring into space and began rambling, "How will I manage this farm without the love of my life? How will I sleep at night? Alvin! Alvin!" And with that she broke down in tears and gut wrenching sobs.

"Nellie, you need to take care of yourself," Morgan told her. She had her arm wrapped securely around Nellie's shoulder and was rubbing her dear friend's arm. "Please, we are family. I will make all the arrangements for you. I will call the casket company in Lexington. I used them when my Andrew passed on. You see, Nellie, I know exactly how you feel right now. I know!!" Morgan held Nellie's hand as they both allowed the tears to flow freely down their cheeks. "I'll be back in a few minutes." Morgan needed to briefly remove herself from the situation. It was bringing back Andrew's death in full force. She needed to stay strong for the Baders and not lose control. She then quietly prayed, "Lord, give me strength to help my family."

The boys knelt at Nellie's feet and patted her hands. With tear-filled eyes, David cried, "Momma, we can take care of you and the farm. We can. Daddy taught us everything we need to know." David wanted Momma to know they were her men.

"My sons, I know you mean well, but there is too much work here. Maybe we might have to move."

Cole spoke up, "Nonsense, Nellie. Morgan and I will see to it you get anything you need, anything at all."

Sunnie sat down beside Nellie with red, teary eyes and hugged her. "I love you, Momma. I love my brothers. We will make it. I know we will." This whole situation was almost too much for Sunnie to bear, but she felt it was important to be there for her momma. After all, she was Daddy's little girl, but watching Momma cry was gut wrenching.

Nellie looked up at Cole. Her eyes and face were red, and tears still streamed down her cheeks. He winked at her and nodded to reassure her that he had meant what he said about Morgan and him providing her with anything she might need.

Alvin's bride was devastated to say the least. How could she go on without him? With her mind racing from one thought to another, Nellie finally remembered that Morgan had gone through the same thing, but without children to comfort and aid her. She and Morgan finally had something in common. They had both lost the love of their lives. This situation, as bad as it was, would draw them even closer.

Morgan returned from the kitchen. "All the arrangements have been made. I took the liberty of calling the Garretts, Mr. Perkins, and Mr. Taylor. The coroner will be here in about fifteen minutes."

"I don't know what I'm supposed to do. What arrangements?" Nellie mumbled, sounding numb.

"My dear, the funeral arrangements. You are too upset. Don't worry about one thing. Now the casket will arrive early Monday morning. You and the children will have a private viewing around one PM. The Garretts or Cole and I can be there for support if you prefer not to be alone. The service will be the following day on Tuesday morning at ten AM."

"This is happening so fast. I don't want to have a funeral. I can't let him go so quickly," Nellie protested, shutting her eyes and shaking her head.

Morgan walked over in front of Nellie and reached down to softly touch her hand. "Sweetie, you can't leave Alvin in the barn forever. I know you want to hold on to him as long as possible, but you can't."

"What would I do without you, Morgan? I'm in shambles. I can't think straight," Nellie told her, looking up at Morgan with a touch of gratitude in her eyes.

"How well I remember," Morgan commented, glancing away and grimacing as pain over her beloved Andrew's death clutched her heart anew.

When the coroner knocked at the door, Nellie struggled to stand in spite of her whole body trembling. She was intent on taking this man to the barn.

"Sit back down, Nellie," Cole said in a kind voice. "I will take this gentleman to Alvin. Please stay here with your family. They need you here." Cole was a take charge kind of a guy. That is why Morgan had him running her farm.

When the men returned to the house, the coroner spoke with Nellie. "It looks as though your husband had a heart attack, ma'am. He went quickly and without much pain. I know this isn't too comforting at the moment, but he did not suffer. I will take the body to be prepared."

"Thank you," Nellie said, swallowing a sob.

"Nellie I am sending a farm hand over to help you out for a couple of months," Morgan instructed.

"Morgan, that won't be necessary. The Garretts will help us. We can manage," Nellie said with more confidence than she felt. Staring blindly into space, she added, "I guess we should try and keep busy; but every turn, every place reminds me of Alvin."

"I understand more than anyone." Morgan said, nodding her head. Her lips were pinched in a hard line. "I still miss Andrew terribly. I promise I will only provide a farmhand for a short while until you get your bearings. Please let me help the only way I know I can." Morgan paused before she added, "Now Dear, don't get angry, but do you need any cash?"

"You are too kind, Morgan, but we have savins' and an insurance policy," Nellie told her.

Pastor Noah let himself in and walked up to Nellie in the parlor. "I'm so very sorry Nellie," he said as he held her hand. His kind, brown eyes relayed his sympathy. "If you don't mind, I would like to read a passage from the Bible and pray." He read the 23rd Psalm, and then he prayed. "Nellie, children, Mrs. Willow has taken care of all the funeral arrangements. You need not worry about a thing," Noah said as he held Nellie's hand again. "If you need someone to talk to, call me. I promise you God will hold you in his hands through all your sorrow."

"Thanks, Pastor Noah. I really need to compose myself enough to call all our relatives," Nellie told him. She arose then and went to call her brother, Bobby, and Alvin's sisters, Cheryl and Alice. It was terribly hard to hold her composure as she talked with each one. After she got off the phone, she held her head and moaned, "I just can't talk anymore. I need to rest. I feel so weak. Sunnie, will you call everyone else?"

Sunnie wanted to take charge. "Momma just lay here on the couch and rest. I'll make some calls while the boys finish what's needed in the barn."

"We all can leave you to rest, or I can stay for awhile if you like," Pastor Noah consoled.

"No, I just want to be alone to rest," she told them all.

"Please don't hesitate to call me or Cole for the slightest need. I do mean this," Morgan stated as she got to her feet and started heading for the front door.

Cole walked over and gave Sunnie a brief hug and a light kiss on the forehead before he followed Morgan out. "Call me if you need anything," he said.

Sunnie merely nodded. She was extremely grateful to have Cole to lean on in this time of sorrow. Knowing he was there for them somehow made it a little more bearable.

After the house was empty, Nellie briefly fell asleep only to awaken to the day's nightmare all over again. It was real. Her Alvin, her best friend, was gone. She would have to learn how to breathe and live all over again.

Monday morning, Lora and Jason, Pastor Noah's daughter and son, prepared the church for Alvin's showing and the funeral. They were in charge of weddings, celebrations, and funerals.

The time had come to say goodbye to Alvin. The first viewing of Alvin was heart-wrenching, but Nellie was determined to be strong. She stood by the casket as the town showed their respect. During this time, Nellie's knees weakened, and she was made to sit in a chair placed by the casket.

Nellie's brother Bobby and his wife Debbie were there. They were staying with Nellie for the time being. Alvin's sisters, Cheryl and Alice, and their husbands Tom and Jerry were also there. They were temporarily staying with Morgan, since Nellie did not have room at her house for everyone to stay.

For Alvin's funeral service the next day, the church was full with not only family but all the neighbors and folks from town. The service was quaint and lovely. Morgan had made sure there were flowers on the casket from Nellie and others from the four children. Officers John and Adam's wives, Lisa and April, sang Alvin's favorite hymn, 'Just As I Am'.

Following the service, the wake was at the Bader farm. The town's people and friends from surrounding farms had sent plenty of food and drinks. Barbara Garrett organized everything for Nellie. After everyone left, Nellie cried and cried. Even though the children sat and cried with her, she felt so alone.

The next days, weeks and months were the most difficult Nellie had ever encountered. She cried herself to sleep almost every night. Nellie hated to admit it, but the farmhand Morgan sent was a godsend. It was just too hard to concentrate on the business at hand. Nellie hoped that time and prayer would eventually heal her deepest sorrow. She kept reminding herself that God doesn't give us a burden too great to bear as she tried to create a new life for her family without her beloved Alvin by her side to guide them all. After all, he had been her rock, her groom, the love of her life.

Chapter 18

It had been months since Alvin's passing. The Bader's tree farm was running smoothly. The boys had really learned how to handle every detail. David told the borrowed farmhand what help was needed. As the boys and Sunnie approached the more difficult chores such as planting and harvesting, they discussed how their daddy would want it done.

That first Christmas after Alvin's death was extremely tough. Nellie knew she must continue the traditions that had been so dear to everyone throughout the years. As usual, extended family members came to visit, but the mood was solemn, instead of joyful. They were comforting to one another. As time passed, Nellie still had her moments as did the siblings, but they were healing.

Finally, Sunnie and the Garrett twins graduated from high school. The Garretts and Baders had a small party for them at the Garrett farm. Morgan, Cole, and Emilio were invited. Sunnie would miss the twins when they went off to U of L. They always listened to her when she shared her thoughts. She would miss all the girl talk.

Sunnie and the twins were in the kitchen gathering more drinks and chips for the buffet table. Sunnie looked at Kim and Kelly with teary eyes. "Girls, you both were so good to me when Daddy died. I couldn't have made it without you.

I'm going to miss you both sooo much. Who will I share my secrets with?"

"Oh, we're sure Cole can handle that," Kim teased. The twins laughed as they hugged Sunnie.

Meanwhile, Jack Garrett, now sixteen, managed to corner Mrs. Willow and talk inquisitively about her horse farm. He had once visited the farm with his sisters. Unlike the Bader boys and their interest in trains, Jack was more like Sunnie with a love of horses. Morgan, being the lady she was, listened with a gentle ear, and kept him in mind for the future.

A month passed, and it was late June. Morgan asked Nellie to come by her farm on her way to town. Nellie briefly thought of the last time she and Alvin were asked to the 'Willow Farm' to discuss a matter. There was no way she could handle a situation like that again....not alone.

Theo showed Nellie to Morgan's office. "How nice it is to see you. Are you doing well? You know I'm still here if you ever need anything at all."

"We are makin' it. At times it is tough, but we have to go on," Nellie replied. Then with nervous curiosity, she cut to the chase, "Now what's this all about, Morgan?"

"As you know, Sunnie has learned all there is about my horse business. I feel in order for her to continue to grow, she should go to the community college in Shelbyville to get an associate's degree in business. This would be two years of study."

"Morgan, you know I can't afford this now!" Nellie lamented, her mouth tense. She was both disappointed and frustrated with her friend.

"I understand. That is why I want to pay *all* of her expenses. I know that Sunnie has saved most of what I have paid her. Perhaps she can purchase her books and supplies, and I'll take care of the tuition. She and I can share the burden, and Shelbyville is close enough for her to commute. She could use your extra vehicle. Alvin bought that nice used truck last year. It should be safe for her to drive."

"There you go again, showin' me up," Nellie complained with a spark of anger in her eyes now. "You've got every detail figured out, don't you?"

"Nellie, calm down. By now, you should know me better than that," Morgan contradicted while frowning. "I look at this as an investment, not a debt. Sunnie could use her degree in many occupations. She would be able to do the bookkeeping for your farm."

"I know. I should be grateful," Nellie stated in a grumble while looking down and rubbing her forehead. Looking Morgan back in the eyes, she admitted, "It's just that I want to be in control sometimes, and I feel like I never have been."

"But woman, you are," Morgan assured her, tapping the desk. "You are running that farm as well as Alvin did, and he taught his children well. They have helped you every step of the way, as they also helped him."

"Okay. Okay. You win!" Nellie replied in an elevated voice, raising her palm up towards Morgan.

"No, we *all* win," Morgan said, and then pointed out, "Sunnie can use the education throughout her life. She in turn can help you and me with our farms," Morgan paused to take a breath and then added, "You and I can go to the college with her when she registers."

"I would like to see this college where my daughter will be studyin'," Nellie told her in a quieter voice as she tried to settle into the idea.

"Nellie, it will be fun. We can make a girls' day trip." Morgan knew the two farms had financial differences, but she wanted the Baders to know that it didn't affect their friendship.

"Okay," Nellie murmured with a reluctant tone. "I will tell Sunnie about your college plans. I'm glad she's been able to stay at home more and help us out. I really needed her."

"Nellie, are you sure you are fine with this? Cole and I love you and your family very much. We just want to help in anyway we can."

"Yes, I know," Nellie accepted, knowing in her heart that Morgan's words were oh so true. "I will get used to the idea," she surrendered in a quiet voice with conceding eyes. Standing, she told Morgan, "Now I'd better get into town."

"Well then, it is all settled," Morgan said with a slight smile. "Try to have a good day, Nellie."

"Goodbye, Morgan," Nellie said as she turned to leave. As she walked toward the front door, Nellie allowed the truth to settle over her. The studies that Morgan was offering could help her daughter become more successful.

When Nellie returned to the farm, she told Sunnie about Morgan's plan for her to get an associate's degree in Shelbyville. Although it wasn't four years of college, it was better than no college at all. Sunnie was finally getting one of her other wishes. She looked forward to studying business courses in order to help keep both farms running smoothly.

Once Sunnie started college, she wasn't able to be at 'Willow Farm' as much. College courses were much harder than high school. She had made some friends in a study group. Bob, Julie, Craig and Shelly were also from farm families. Paying college tuition was a financial sacrifice for farmers. The group had things in common. Bob's dad had also passed away. Craig was dry-witted and kept them all laughing when things got too tense. The study group did help the time to pass ever so quickly. Sunnie really enjoyed their friendship.

One Saturday, Sunnie was in Cole's office going on and on about the new friends she had made at college. When she talked of Julie and Shelly, he didn't seem to mind. But when Sunnie mentioned Bob and Craig and the things she had in common with them, Cole grew very quiet and got a funny expression on his face.

"Is something wrong, Cole?" Sunnie asked him.

"No," he said, shaking his head. "Nothing's wrong," he told her, placing both his hands in his pockets and leaning on the desk. Sunnie was going to college now, and she was past eighteen. If he did not pursue a relationship with her, then one of the boys she was making friends with at school was likely to. He might possibly lose his Sunnie forever. With this in mind, Cole cleared his throat and said, "Sunnie, I think it's time I make my intentions known to you."

"Your....intentions?" she questioned and frowned. She was a bit concerned now. Was Cole angry with her about something?

"Sunnie, you know I care about you a great deal," he told her with his eyes warmly holding hers.

"I care about you too," she admitted, giggling. She was not used to having such serious conversations with Cole.

"That being said, I think it's time we....we um....dated," Cole said with a happy face and bright eyes. It was hard to get that statement out, but he finally did it.

Sunnie's forehead wrinkled again as she blurted, "Date each other?" They had jokingly flirted some, but there was that age difference. It was imperative that they were completely professional at 'Willow Farm'.

"Yes. We can go into Lexington or Louisville to movies, plays, ball games, you know...date. This will give us an opportunity to get to know one another outside the farm," Cole further explained. "So what do you say, young lady? Can I have the honor of your presence tonight? How does dinner and a movie sound?"

Sunnie's face brightened as she eagerly told him, "Dinner and a movie sounds great, Cole! I need to tell Momma that you want to date me."

"Of course you do," he agreed. "I hope she will approve. We also need to let Ms. Morgan know too," he said, grinning ear to ear. Cole released the desk and placed his hands upon Sunnie's shoulders. "You've made me very happy, Sunnie. I think we are going to enjoy dating."

"I think so too," Sunnie told him, excited beyond reason. She had always secretly dreamed that someday she and Cole would date, and now he was making another dream come true.

So Sunnie and Cole began to date, with the blessings of both her momma and Ms. Morgan. Because Sunnie was so busy working both the farms and going to school, she and Cole did not get to date as much as they might have liked, but they still went out on occasion.

Cole took this new relationship with Sunnie very slowly. When they went out, he held her hand and opened doors for her. When he took her home, he ended each date with a quick kiss on the cheek. He was still very aware of the age difference between them and did not want Sunnie, her momma, or Ms. Morgan to disapprove in any way. They were enjoying their time together and getting to know each other away from the business atmosphere.

Time passed quickly and before Sunnie knew it her second year of studies was coming to an end. She was nearing twenty. The twins had met up with Sunnie's cousins, Tim and Steve, at U of L. They had been running around together as a group. Eventually Kim started dating Tim, and Steve started dating Kelly. Sunnie trusted her cousins. They were honorable men. They had better be or they would hear from her! Thinking of her best friends dating her favorite boy cousins put a smile on Sunnie's face. It was almost as perfect as her and Cole.

On one special Saturday morning, Sunnie was in Cole's office. After they finished a conversation about a new client, he did what he had been so patiently waiting for. He pulled her into him tightly and gave her a hug. "I love you Sunnie. You should know that," he confessed all at once.

"I love you too Cole. I love everyone here." Deep inside, Sunnie had waited so long for this, but she wasn't completely sure Cole felt the same way. She had loved Cole for a long time and wanted to make sure it wasn't just puppy love.

"I know you love everyone here, but my love is one that a man has for a woman."

"Yes, I know," she said shyly as she briefly looked down. Then looking Cole straight in his eyes she said, "I love you as a woman loves a man. So what do we do now?"

Morgan had heard the end of this conversation as she entered the office. "*Well, well*, we have strange expressions on our faces. Do you two care to share with me?" she said slowly with her head tilted down and her eyes looking upward.

"Ms. Morgan, I'll let you in on a little secret," Cole said. His eyes were twinkling with mischief. "If this beautiful young lady will have me, I really want to marry her."

Sunnie shouted with her hands on her hips, "Cole, Cole! You could have asked me first. It's my hand you are asking for."

Morgan spoke up, "You both know I approve, but I strongly suggest you ask Nellie and her sons for Sunnie's hand. She doesn't need to feel another loss, but rather that she has gained a son.

Sunnie interrupted these two connivers. "Excuse me! Excuse me! You both are assuming I will say yes."

Cole pulled a beautiful ring out of his pocket that he purchased a few weeks ago. He was waiting for just the right moment. He would never accept 'no' for an answer.

The ring took Sunnie's breath away. "Cole, did you pick this out by yourself?"

"Most certainly. I had it designed just for you."

Morgan grinned as she slowly strolled closer to get a good look. With her arms folded and peering over Sunnie's arm, she said quietly, "Not bad, Cole; not bad at all. You have excellent taste."

"Yes ma'am," Cole said anxiously hoping for a 'YES'. "Sunnie, I'm waiting. What is your answer?"

With tear-filled eyes, Sunnie looked at Cole, and blurted, "Yes, yes, yes! *I will* marry you!"

Cole placed the ring on Sunnie's finger, and she hugged and kissed him. She then turned and hugged Morgan.

"I'm so happy. This would not have happened if it wasn't for you, Ms. Morgan."

"Well, that makes me feel good. Now, off with the both of you. Go to Nellie and the boys. Oh, I almost forgot." She turned to Sunnie, "Jack Garrett showed some interest in horses at your graduation party two years ago. As a matter of fact, he talked my ear off that day. David and he are still good friends are they not?"

"Yes, they are. Why do you ask?"

"As you both know, we are losing Jose'. We need someone to replace him. Perhaps Jack would like to work here. Sunnie, you could take him under your wing as I did you."

"We will go to the Garretts after speaking to my family."

For Sunnie, the ride to the Bader farm seemed more like an hour rather than minutes. When they arrived, Sunnie gathered her brothers from the back yard. "Guys, Cole and I have something important to discuss with you and Momma. Please come inside." Nellie was baking bread.

Nellie wiped her hands with the towel, and then placed the dough into the oven. "You're home early. Cole, what a pleasant surprise. What's up?"

"Everyone, we have something to tell you. Please sit down," Cole instructed.

The Baders slowly sat down at the kitchen table with faces showing a bit of concern and confusion.

"Nellie, boys," Cole said with a sheepish expression while running his hands around his cowboy hat. "I wish to ask for Sunnie's hand in marriage."

Jonas asked, "You want to marry her hand?" He was joking and tried to get a rise out of Cole.

Cole laughed, "Jonas, when a man wishes to marry a woman, it is proper and fitting that he ask the father's permission. Since Alvin's passing, I thought it would be appropriate to ask the men of the house and Sunnie's mother.

"You want to marry *her*?" Ethan said as he curled up his lip.

Cole took Sunnie's hands and looked lovingly into her eyes. "Yes, she's the love of my life." Then chuckling, he turned to Nellie and said, "Nellie, you can close your mouth now."

"Well, I....I don't know what to say," she said with a look of wonder and amazement.

"Say yes. After all, you will be getting another son.... *me*," he said, tapping his chest.

"What did Sunnie say about this?"

"I said yes, Momma. Yes, yes, yes!" Sunnie exclaimed with a gleaming smile, looking from Nellie to the man she loved oh so much.

"Well...if that's the case, then...yes it is," Nellie agreed, a wide smile also gracing her face. "Congratulations to you both," she said, reaching to embrace Sunnie and then also giving Cole a welcoming hug. Nellie had always admired Cole for being such a kind, helpful man. She knew from talking to Sunnie that he had been a perfect gentleman on their dates as well. Nellie would be happy to have such a fine man as a son-in-law.

Sunnie couldn't hide her huge diamond any longer. She nonchalantly scratched her nose.

"Gosh, you are blindin' me with that thing." Sunnie's ring contained the largest diamond Nellie had ever seen.

Sunnie grinned as she stuck her hand up to Momma. "Isn't it just the most beautiful thing you've ever seen?"

"No, sweetheart, you are the most beautiful thing I've ever seen....my beautiful, grown-up daughter. Oh, if your daddy could just see you now," Nellie said, a wave of sadness passing over her. But the sadness passed quickly because Nellie felt deep down that Alvin was present and would never miss his daughter's wedding.

"Wow, another brother. You have *our* permission too." David finally chimed in, speaking for all the men of the house.

"Thank you, new brothers." Cole said with a grateful grin and a bow of his head. He wanted the boys to feel it was just as important to get their approval as it was their mother's.

David, Ethan, and Jonas took turns hugging Sunnie and shaking Cole's hand.

"Have you guys set a date?" Nellie asked, curious about the details.

"We want to be engaged for awhile, since we just shared our true feelings for each other. Besides, we really haven't had a chance to date all that much," Cole informed them.

"Where will you live, who will pay for this weddin'?" Curiosity was really getting to Nellie. She wasn't sure she could handle these expenses.

"We will worry about these matters later." Cole assured Nellie.

"Does Morgan know?"

"Yes Momma. She came in on our conversation. She is very happy for us."

"I would expect so. I'm sure this *made her* day," Nellie said sarcastically.

"Momma, do I hear some sarcasm in your voice? That is so not like you."

"I know," Nellie said with a sheepish look on her face. "Morgan's been such a big part of your life and a good friend to me, but for her to find out first.....well," Nellie uttered in a quiet voice with downcast eyes. Then recovering from her brief spell of jealousy, she said, "Oh don't mind me. I'm bein' selfish and jealous. You two enjoy your engagement."

"Momma, you and my brothers are a very important part of my life too. I love you all very much. Our closeness will never change," Sunnie assured her, draping an arm around Nellie's shoulder and giving her a kiss on the cheek.

"You are right, my sweet daughter. I wish Alvin was here to sing 'Daddy's Little Girl' for you again."

"I have missed that every birthday since he died," Sunnie admitted, looking down at her feet as a trace of pain touched her heart. "He was the best father in the world."

"And the best husband," Nellie said, squeezing Sunnie's hand and flashing a bittersweet smile.

"Momma, we really need to go," Sunnie told her, even though she hated to separate from her family while she was feeling low. "Morgan wants us to speak with Jack Garrett about working at 'Willow Farm'. He had expressed interest to her at my graduation party."

"Well, off with you," Nellie said, releasing Sunnie's hand and flashing a smile. With a giggle, she added, "And don't forget to show off that rock you have. Ha, ha."

"Cole and I are going to celebrate our engagement. So don't look for me until late tonight," Sunnie told her with a wink and a happy smile.

"As you should," Nellie agreed.

"See you guys later," David said. Ethan and Jonas bid them farewell too. Then Cole and Sunnie headed for the door.

Nellie and Alvin's daughter had finally grown up. It was a sad and happy time of letting go and gaining a family member. Nellie didn't want to even think of her sons leaving home.

After speaking with Mr. Garrett and Jack about working at the horse farm, Jack accepted the offer. Sunnie wasn't surprised. She knew Jack shared her love for those gorgeous creatures. Jack would be an asset to the farm. She was sure of it.

Of course, Sunnie couldn't leave without showing off her ring. The Garretts were good family friends. They were so happy for Sunnie and Cole. They also suspected their twins were getting serious with their boyfriends too.

Barbara blurted, "Sunnie those cousins of yours, Tim and Steve, seem to be fine young men. So far, we are impressed."

"They had better be good to my two best friends, or they will hear from me. I instructed them to be perfect gentlemen," Sunnie laughed knowing they had been raised to be just that.

Later that evening, the engaged couple made it official by getting all dressed up and going to a rather expensive restaurant in Louisville for dinner. Cole was Sunnie's first love and would be her only husband. She knew this love would last forever. It had been growing for oh so long.

Chapter 19

It was late spring. Sunnie had done well with her studies. She was nearing twenty-one and had an associate's degree in accounting and business. Momma was so very proud. She realized that if it wasn't for Morgan, Sunnie would not have been able to get this degree. Nellie felt bad about ever doubting Morgan's intentions. Her brother Bobby was the only other one in the family that had some college.

David was nineteen, Ethan seventeen, and Jonas was fifteen. They had grown up quickly because of Alvin's death. Although, Nellie made all the final decisions, her sons knew all there was to know about tree farming, vegetable gardening, and preparing the animals for table food. Sunnie's degree did come in handy for keeping the books and running the business. These were things Alvin had always done and had learned from Ernest.

There were times the Bader family also needed Sunnie to help take an animal to slaughter or to cut trees. She still wanted to be a big part of the farm's operation. Morgan still occasionally provided a strong man for the difficult and heavy jobs.

Sunnie had been groomed well. She knew every aspect of the horse business. There also had been many Derbys attended and many opportunities to meet jockeys, trainers, and such.

One Sunday morning after church as the Baders pulled into their driveway, Cole was waiting. Something was wrong. He looked as though he had lost his best friend.

Sunnie quickly jumped out of the vehicle and slammed the door. She went running up to him. "Cole, darling, what is wrong? What is the matter?" Sunnie questioned as the rest of the Baders followed her. "Why weren't you and Ms. Morgan at church today?"

He made gestures with his hands towards the house and said, "Let's go inside. I have something to tell you all." They all went into the kitchen, "Please, everyone sit down. Something terrible has happened."

"What, what is it. Cole, tell us. What is it?" Sunnie was afraid to even guess.

Cole sunk his hands down into the pocket of his jeans, averted his eyes from his beautiful Sunnie's, took a deep breath, and carefully revealed, "I'm so sorry to have to tell you all this but....Morgan has passed on. Theo found her in bed this morning. The coroner said she must have had a stroke."

Sunnie eyes grew large and her lips trembled as she cried out, "No, no, this can't be! I can't lose someone else I love. I can't!! What are we going to do? I just can't believe it. I thought Morgan would live forever. I've learned so much from her. I need to go to her."

Sunnie got up to dart out the door. Cole grabbed her by the arm. She turned toward him. He embraced her, and she cried like a baby, sobbing brokenheartedly as the tears wet his shirt.

Nellie's eyes filled with tears. She and Morgan had become such good friends in spite of Morgan's strong and convincing ways. Morgan was the only one that understood what it was like to lose a husband. She was the one who constantly encouraged Nellie to go on, telling her that she would persevere. "What should we do, Cole?" she asked him. "We want to help."

"We know how to run a farm," Ethan spoke up. "We can help with the horse farm now." Ethan was such a sweetheart.

Cole took charge. "Everyone calm down," he said, shaking his hands palms down. "There is nothing to do. Ms. Morgan was an efficient and great business woman. She had provisions in place for every scenario."

"Whatever do you mean?" Nellie asked with a look of confusion in her eyes.

"Her body is on its way to Lexington where the service will be," Cole informed them.

"Lexington! She belongs here! My teacher and friend belongs here!" Sunnie shouted with disagreement.

"Now think about it, Sunnie," Cole said in a soothing, even-tempered voice. "Morgan has so many friends, clients and colleagues. Neither her farm nor the church could hold all these people. The service will be held at the church she attended there; then she will be laid to rest next to Andrew. These arrangements have been in place since Andrew's passing."

It was hard for David, Ethan and Jonas to see their sister hurting again. It was different this time. This time they couldn't take charge. They could only comfort her as best they knew how.

Nellie looked at Sunnie and Cole. She saw two broken hearts. "You must be a support system for each other and to the farmhands."

"That is a given, Nellie," Cole assured her. "I don't know all the details, but Ms. Morgan had told me she made provisions for the farm to continue if anything were to happen to her. I need to get back there and reassure everyone."

With a broken heart and red, tear-filled eyes Sunnie added, "I'll go with you. All those guys loved working for Ms. Morgan. They really respected her."

Another death, life just wasn't fair. Nellie had become dependent on Morgan's encouragement. Morgan was the strong woman that Nellie wanted to resemble.

When the time came, the people of Pleasureville and surrounding farms met and rode together to Lexington to pay respects to a woman who had been kind to all. Pastor Noah had been asked to give her eulogy.

Leaving the church in Lexington, the funeral precession went as far down the road as the eye could see. Most of the horse farm owners from Lexington were there as well as clients, colleagues, and most of Pleasureville and Henry County.

Next to Daddy's death, this was the hardest thing Sunnie had ever experienced. It was almost as bad as losing her daddy. Her heart was broken again. She had been Daddy's little girl. Coming back to Pleasureville from the funeral, she reflected on the song, 'Daddy's Little Girl', that Alvin sang to her on every birthday. This recollection brought tears to her eyes. The special song her daddy had always sung to her was a memory she would treasure always. Cole tightly held Sunnie's hand, but said nothing. He knew she needed to grieve, and so did he. It was too hard to think beyond today. The 'Willow Farm' or its future was far from anyone's mind on this sad day.

The friendship and mentor both Cole and Sunnie had had in Morgan would always be treasured by them both. They would greatly miss their dear friend, but they knew she was in a better place.... in the arms of the Lord. Cole was grateful to Sunnie for reminding him to keep Jesus in his life. Their faith brought comfort to the couple in Morgan's passing.

Chapter 20

Many weeks passed. It was time for the reading of the Will. It was nine o'clock in the morning. Sunnie, Nellie, the boys, and Pastor Noah were asked to come to 'Willow Farm'. Nellie had no idea why she and her sons were beckoned. Perhaps Morgan was leaving her an antique. She was bewildered and wondered why on earth she would want the boys there. Morgan also requested all the farm employees to be present and the pastor from her Lexington church.

Folding chairs had been placed throughout the great room to accommodate seating. Everyone quietly gathered in anticipation. Ms. Willow's lawyer, Kevin Merken, was short and in his mid-forties. He had a receding hair line and a mustache. Although few knew it, Mr. Merken was one of the best lawyers money could buy. He was wearing, what appeared to be, an expensive suit. He thanked everyone for coming. Then in a baritone voice that echoed and stirred everyone in the room, he began to read "The Last Will and Testament of Morgan Elizabeth Willow…." He first read the preliminary details of the will, that Mrs. Willow was of sane mind, and so on. He went on to announce, "I do hereby solely appoint Cole Wade Lawson as the Executor of my estate both real and personal." Cole was given this information soon after his employer's death because of the many details that needed to be attended to. He glanced at Sunnie with a grin. She smiled at him and squeezed his hand, knowing Morgan had made the right choice. Cole would do a good job executing Morgan's Will.

Mr. Merken came to the part where provisions were made:

● "To all I am about to mention, you have been blessings to me. My life would have been less joyful had it not been for every one of you. I leave you words from one of my favorite hymns. *'Whatsoever you do to the least of my brothers that you do unto me'.*"

● "To my loyal farmhands who work so diligently, I leave each one $25,000, and hope you will continue to work at 'Willow Farm'."

Because Jack Garrett was a new farmhand, he certainly was surprised and grateful that he was included. Sunnie gave him a smile, noticing the shocked expression on his face. Jack had not been around long enough to know about Ms. Morgan's kind and generous spirit. They all listened as Morgan's attorney continued to read:

● "To Emilio, my farm would not be what it is today without you. I leave you $100,000, and hope that you will continue as the assistant manager at 'Willow Farm'."

Now, it was Emilio's turn to look shocked. Thinking he would be getting $25,000, he lowered his head and fought tears of gratitude. He knew he would miss Mrs. Willow a great deal. She had been a grand lady, and a wonderful person to work for. He intended to stay on at 'Willow Farm' and see that it continued to operate with excellence as she would have expected.

● "To Theo and Oliver, you both have been loyal employees and family members. I leave you each $100,000 and hope that you will continue at 'Willow Farm'."

Theo and Oliver glanced at one another and shared a bittersweet smile as Theo gave Oliver a pat on the shoulder. They both knew they would continue on at 'Willow Farm' as well, in loving tribute to their employer, who had been family to them.

At this point, there was slight chatter in the room, but Mr. Merken asked everyone to be quiet until he was finished. He cleared his throat and continued:

● "To David, Ethan, and Jonas, I leave you each $15,000. I only ask that you use it for your education.

David was sitting to Nellie's right. Jonas and Ethan were to her left. David looked at Momma as did Jonas and Ethan. All were leaning out looking at one another with total shock. Nellie started to tear up, but placed her forefinger to her lips to keep her sons from speaking out.

● "To Southland Christian Church in Lexington, Kentucky, I leave $100,000."

● "To Henry County Christian Church, I leave $100,000."

Pastor Noah gasped out loud. He had never expected Morgan to be so overly generous. This large amount would do a lot for his small church.

● "To my dear friends, Nellie and Sunnie, I
leave you both my jewelry in equal shares,
share and share alike."

Sunnie looked over at Momma and gave her a warm
smile. She thought how pretty Momma would look in some of
Ms. Morgan's jewelry. Her heart was swelling with love for
Ms. Morgan, for all she was doing now, and for all she had
done for her family in the past.

● "To my dearest friend, Nellie, I leave you
$50,000 to use as you see fit. Hopefully the
tree farm will be passed down to your boys."

Despite her restraint, Nellie gasped. She placed a hand
over her mouth and the tears that she had been silently fighting
began to stream down her cheeks. In these times, it was
becoming harder to hold onto a farm, and this money would
surely come in handy.

David placed his arm around Momma and gave her a
consoling squeeze. Morgan was still taking care of him and
his family, even though she was no longer amidst them. What
a grand lady she was!

● "And finally to Cole and Sunnie, I leave
you both in equal shares, share and share alike,
the 'Willow Farm', my home, its contents, and
my Rolls Royce. The remainder of my estate
will be in trust for the operation of the farm and
house."

Sunnie grabbed Cole's arm and started to cry. She
looked at him in bewilderment. Cole looked shocked as well.

Everyone in the room was dumbfounded and sitting
there with their mouths open. Morgan's lawyer had a great
sense of humor. "Okay, everyone, you can all close your

mouths now. Morgan was a generous lady, a giving person. Let us feel proud and blessed that she touched all of our lives. The 'Willow Farm' is to continue business as usual. The probate should be completed inside a year. Now, if you will excuse me, I have another appointment." He personally shook everyone's hand and thanked them again for coming. When he took Cole's hand he said, "There is much for you to do. You need to go into court with me and be sworn in as Executor. Morgan's bank accounts have been closed. You will have to open another account for the estate with your name in order to pay expenses on the estate. There also will be a lot of papers for you to sign. I will call you as soon as we have a court date."

"I understand, Mr. Merken. I have never been an Executor before. I'm not sure I know just what to do," he admitted with a bit of a lost expression on his face. For the first time, Cole was unsure of himself. He couldn't get his thoughts wrapped around the task at hand.

"That is what I'm here for, to lead you through it all," Mr. Merken assured Cole. "I'll be back in touch very soon." Then he turned and slowly made his way out of the house.

Nellie was flabbergasted. She turned to Sunnie and Cole. "I can't believe she left me, David, Ethan, and Jonas money. It never crossed my mind even when we were asked to come to the reading. I thought perhaps she had left me a piece of jewelry or an antique."

"She loved the whole family, Momma," Sunnie told her while giving Nellie a small hug.

Cole was only half listening. He had one other important item of a very personal nature on his mind. With his take-charge demeanor finally taking over, Cole got up, grabbed Sunnie's hand and pulled her as he walked in front of the fireplace. He cleared his throat. "Excuse me. May I have everyone's attention? I think there is one other matter that needs to be attended to here today." He turned to Sunnie and said, "I think, young lady that a wedding is now in order. After all, the house will be in both our names. It would not be proper for us to live here unless we are married. Don't you all agree?"

With that, everyone clapped and whistled. "Yes, yes, a wedding!" they all shouted.

David was standing next to his brothers and Momma. He said with a joking smile, "Well guys, we finally are getting rid of miss bossy."

Jonas added while pointing to his brothers, "Don't worry, Momma. Your men can take very good care of you and the farm." They all busted out in laugher, needing some humor to lighten things up a bit.

"I would be glad to do the honors," Pastor Noah spoke up. "Shall we set the date?"

Cole turned to Sunnie who was beaming with joy and crying at the same time. "You pick the date, my love."

"It takes time to plan a wedding…. I'm not sure."

"Let's keep it small, our farm family, your family and a few friends. That should make it easier. I know the ladies in this county will be more than happy to help."

"I feel strange asking these ladies to help." Sunnie didn't want to impose on anyone.

Noah spoke up. "I think it is more than fitting to get them involved. They have helped with other weddings in the county. I can always count on them with church functions. They can handle it. Just assign each a task and deadline. It will get done."

Nellie reminded Sunnie, "Your fiancé is waiting for a date, my dear."

"Oh, okay. Let's see….I think, ah. How about May 25th?" Sunnie was originally planning a 'couples' get together with Tim, Kim, Steve, and Kelly on this particular Saturday, but getting married seemed like a better idea.

"Then it is settled. Saturday, May 25th you will become Mrs. Cole Lawson," Cole shouted. With that, every-one clapped and congratulated them.

While they talked amongst themselves, the gathered group, including Sunnie's brothers, slowly dissipated. They all had tasks to attend to. After all had left, Cole asked his bride-to-be, and soon to be mother-in-law, to sit down for a minute. "You women can plan this wedding as you see fit, but there are two things that I plan to do. All, and I do mean *all*, expenses are to be paid by me. There will be no further discussions about the financing of this great event. I will also take care of the honeymoon arrangements. Understood?" Cole had saved all his life for something special.

"But the bride's family...." Nellie knew it was proper etiquette for her to pay for the wedding.

"Nellie, I said this subject is not open for discussion. Case closed." There, again was his take-charge demeanor.

Nellie surrendered and hugged Cole. "Yes sir."

"One other thing, Sunnie. We both should get passports just in case we wander out of the country."

"Whatever you say, my love." Sunnie could have questioned her fiancé about this, but chose to let him handle his plans without interference.

The bride put her arm around her mother. "Momma, we will have plenty to do. Now let's go home. I want to talk more to my brothers. I'm sure they are so excited that Morgan left them each a gift, and I know they will enjoy taking care of you after I'm married. Maybe this afternoon we can make a list of wedding tasks and make some calls. We only have a couple of months to pull this shindig off."

Before Sunnie and Nellie hurried off, Sunnie embraced Cole and gave him a kiss. Then, she turned back to Momma. "Mother of the bride, let's go start planning my wedding."

Chapter 21

The next two months passed quickly. The numerous tasks were attended to in great detail thanks to everyone's help. At times, Nellie and Sunnie could barely catch their breath, but the wedding plans were coming together very nicely.

Kim and Kelly were both maids of honor and played a big part in the wedding preparations as did Barbara Garrett. They had given Sunnie a shower at their farm where she received a lot of nice gifts. The twins also shared some exciting news with the bride. It seems they both were engaged too. In three months, Kim was to marry Sunnie's cousin Tim. Kelly and Steve were to wed six months thereafter. These life-long friends had shared everything. They now would be a big part of each other's weddings. Just how much joy could one person stand? They all were ecstatically happy and blessed.

As expected, many ladies of Pleasureville had specific tasks for the wedding, such as Anna Rose who helped Sunnie with her music selection. Barbara Garrett made the decorations for the reception. Mr. Taylor's wife had worked in a floral shop at one time and offered to make all the flower arrangements and boutonnières. She ordered the flowers from the Derby City.

The help Nellie and Sunnie received from so many great people was such a relief for the Bader women. They gave all the helpful women gold, cross necklaces as a big thank you for their enormous helpfulness. Cole gave gifts to Emilio,

Theo, Oliver and Sunnie's brothers as well. They received pocket watches. Since Cole didn't have much family, Emilio was to be his best man. Theo and Oliver had played a big part in preparing the food and drinks for the reception, which would take place at 'Willow Farm'.

Of course, all of Sunnie's relatives were in town for the celebration. They wouldn't miss this for the world, especially Tim and Steve. After all, they needed pointers for their upcoming nuptials.

Barbara Garrett and Nellie helped their girls dress in the church's back meeting room. It wouldn't be long before Nellie would be helping with the Garrett weddings. Sunnie was a beautiful bride. She had chosen a cream, off-the-shoulder, beaded dress which hugged her figure and enhanced her olive complexion. The gown had a short train. Atop her head was a beaded, cream cap that had a short veil. Her beaded shoes matched the dress. Sunnie's blue garter was borrowed from a school friend. Nellie had given her daughter the pearl earrings she wore as a bride. Sunnie carried a bouquet of cream roses.

Nellie had never dressed so elegantly. She had on a lovely, pink, silk suit with silver shoes. Her corsage was of cream & pink roses. Nellie had chosen pearl earrings from Morgan's collection.

The twins wore simple, long, fuchsia sheath dresses with fuchsia crocheted shawls. They carried cream and fuchsia roses. They had found all their gowns at a bridal shop in Louisville. Cole wore a cream tux with a fuchsia vest. Emilio had on a black tux with a fuchsia vest. David, Ethan, and Jonas wore black tuxes with cream vests. Cole's boutonniere was fuchsia. The remaining men had cream roses for their boutonnières.

As usual, Pastor Noah's daughter and son, Lora and Jason, had prepared the church for the wedding. The Henry County Christian Church was packed. Sunnie wanted all of her brothers to give her away. David walked a few steps in front of Sunnie while Ethan and Jonas flanked her sides. As she slowly descended down the aisle, Anna Rose played a lovely rendition of 'Here Comes the Bride' on the organ. Cole's breath was taken away by the sight of his beautiful bride, and a tear fell from his eye. He loved Sunnie more than life itself.

The ceremony was so lovely. It indeed was the most beautiful wedding the county had ever seen. Nellie's eyes were filled with tears of joy. Cole was a wonderful man. There was no doubt he would take good care of her daughter and make her happy.

Even though David was a grown man of nineteen now, he briefly wiped a tear from his cheek. He didn't want anyone to see, but he truly loved his sister. It was now up to him and his brothers to take care of Momma.

After pictures were taken, Oliver drove the newlyweds to 'Willow Farm' in the Rolls Royce. Both would soon belong to the couple. Everyone seemed to be enjoying themselves at the reception. Very few people in the area had been to 'Willow Farm'. So as they entered the *estate*, a lot of ooohs and ahhhs could be heard. Not only had Mrs. Willow been a pillar of the community, but the Baders were now a family of great stature. Everyone was glad to be a part of this happy event.

Sunnie had invited her college study group. It was so good to see Bob, Julie, Craig and Shelly again, and they were very happy to meet her new husband and see her new home. The bride and groom chatted with the study group of which Craig was the jokester. He said while twirling his forefinger, "Well, you've done alright for yourself babes. Do you have extra bedrooms? We all want to move in." This brought out laughter with those gathered.

Sunnie had a come-back and said with a smirk, "We'll start construction tomorrow. We will have to add on if you all come here to live. Now if you guys will excuse me, I need to thank my men in the kitchen." With that, she hugged everyone and Cole shook their hands.

As the bride and groom walked away, Shelly leaned into Julie and boasted, "Our girl friend has done alright for herself. That Cole is a real looker. She had mentioned a few things about this place, but nothing like it really is. Can you imagine living here?" Julie nodded back as not to draw attention from Bob and Craig. They would not understand girl-talk. Sunnie's friends were very happy for her.

The bride went into the kitchen where Theo and Oliver were standing. "We could not have done this without you both. Thank you so very much for everything," she said, giving them each a hug and kiss on the cheek.

"You are most welcome, Mrs. Lawson," Theo said with a smile and a twinkle in his eye. He was very happy for Sunnie and glad that she and Cole had decided to marry.

Sunnie returned Theo's smile, saying, "Well...now... that is a name I'll have to get used to, but please continue to call me Sunnie. We are family now."

"Yes ma'am. Welcome to our family," said Theo as Oliver nodded.

"You need not worry about the food expenses. That is our gift to you both," Oliver added.

"How ever did you get Cole to agree to that?"

Theo stated, "I simply explained to him that preparing food was my area of expertise and that Oliver and I wanted the food to be our gift to you both. He finally conceded."

Touched, Sunnie hugged Theo and Oliver again, saying, "I love you guys." Her warm words made their day.

Cole came into the kitchen looking for his bride. "Oliver, Theo, please follow me," he said as he escorted Sunnie to the fireplace. "Everyone, may I have your attention. My lovely bride still does not know where we are honeymooning." He turned and clutched Sunnie's hands as he looked into her eyes. "Darling, tomorrow, Oliver is taking us to the airport in Louisville. From there we are going to travel throughout Italy."

Everyone gasped as they clapped and cheered. This lovely, sunny lady who was now Mrs. Cole Wade Lawson was going to Europe for the first time.

"Italy? Really?!" Sunnie asked, her whole face beaming with happiness.

"Really," Cole told her, draping an arm around her waist and pulling her to him for a kiss. "Are you happy, Mrs. Lawson?"

This time the reference of this name did not seem so strange to Sunnie. In fact, it seemed to fit her to a tee, as if she should have always had this name. "I'm the happiest woman in the world, Cole!" Sunnie gushed, giving him another few, excited pecks on the lips.

"Good. Because that's the way I want you to always feel," he told her, his eyes glowing with the deepest of love. He felt like the luckiest man in the world.

The party continued for awhile. Everyone seemed to be enjoying themselves. The wedding couple tried to talk with every guest. Eventually, the group slowly left the horse farm.

Nellie kissed both Sunnie and Cole with tears falling down her face. Each brother gave Cole a firm hand shake while asking him to take very good care of their only sister. Cole promised with all his heart to do just that.

It was nearing ten PM. Theo and Oliver had decorated the master suite with new silk bedding and plenty of candles. Theo walked up to the couple. "You both have had a very busy day. Oliver and I will clean things up. I think you both should retire. You have another big day tomorrow with your traveling plans." Cole shook Theo's hand and thanked him. Theo received a very tight hug and a kiss from Sunnie.

The following day, the Baders and all of the visiting relatives came to 'Willow Farm' to join in bidding farewell to the newlyweds. Everyone stood under the portico and waved them on as the Rolls pulled away and headed toward the airport. This was a new adventure on a plane that would take them to Italy, fulfilling yet another of Sunnie's dreams.

Chapter 22

Cole had instructed the travel agent to reserve the bridal suite in every hotel which included flowers, candles, and champagne. It was sooo beautiful and romantic. Cole also carried his bride over every suite's threshold. He lovingly and continually referred to her as his bride. Cole loved Sunnie so much that he knew in his heart that she would always be his bride. This was so surprising to Sunnie since her Daddy had sometimes referred to Momma as his bride.

Sunnie hoped that their marriage would be as wonderful as Momma and Daddy's. Her parents had been such great role models not only as a couple, who ran a business well together, but also as a man and woman that truly loved one another.

During the next two weeks, Cole and Sunnie traveled extensively throughout Italy. The newlyweds managed to visit the Sistine Chapel and view Michelangelo's paintings and hear the interesting story behind them. Of course, they couldn't miss St. Peter's Cathedral. The vastness of this church contained mini chapels and such beautiful sculptures along with St. Peter's tomb. It was such a spiritual experience. They also visited a museum and viewed the famous statue of David.

In Florence, there was also much to see. They had fun buying many Italian leather gifts for family and friends. Cole bought his bride her own Italian leather purse.

The gypsies were quite a site to behold. They had a knack of working in twos with one occupying their prey while the other would pick-pocket or grab a purse. If they asked for money and got nothing, they would sometimes spit at people. The newlyweds were a little flabbergasted by these unusual people.

Cole thought a train ride would be a quaint experience. So they took a train to Sicily. On this island off of Italy, there were peasant-like villages, but with unique shopping and food. Sleeping in a birth was definitely an unusual experience for the couple, but the bathrooms were very tight quarters with barely enough room to shower. They were rocked to sleep by the swaying of the train as it clickity-clacked down the track. The food on the train was surprisingly good. In Italy, most people rode scooters, bikes or drove very tiny cars. It was amazing to learn so much from this culture. And oh how divine was the food. All in all, this trip was one to remember.

As their honeymoon, and trip overseas, came to an end, Sunnie started to pack the suitcases as Cole pulled a few things from the closet. "I want to create an album of pictures and a travel log of all the sites of this trip. Everyone will enjoy looking at it, and we can show it to our kids," Sunnie stated.

"That's a fantastic idea. We don't ever want to forget this trip. It would be great if we could plan trips for milestone anniversaries. What do you think?" Cole added while checking the chest of drawers.

"I'm all for that, my love," Sunnie agreed, smiling with utmost approval. Sunnie stopped packing for a moment and sat on the bed. "I've really enjoyed myself on this trip, but I will be ever so glad to get to my new home."

"Excuse me. You mean *our* new home," Cole corrected with a chuckle.

"I have to get used to it being *our* new home," Sunnie laughed, swinging her legs back and forth like an excited child.

"Well if I have anything to do with it, you'll have years and years to get used to it," Cole told her, coming over and giving her a loving kiss. He looked forward to going home and settling into their new life as well.

The next morning, it was time to return home to their farm and get on to business. There were also two more weddings to plan. It was sad to leave Italy, but living on the horse farm was something to look forward to, especially for Sunnie.

Oliver picked up the couple at the Louisville airport and drove the newlyweds home to Pleasureville. "We missed you both. How was your trip?" he asked, looking back at them in the rear-view mirror.

"Oh, Oliver it was grand! It was great being out of the country. Once I finish our trip album, I will show Theo and you all the sites," Sunnie explained as her face glowed with contentment.

Oliver glanced back in the mirror. He couldn't help but smile as he saw the couple clinging to each other in the back seat. As they drove up to the portico, Cole said, "Well my bride, we are home."

After Oliver opened the back door of their Rolls, Cole got out and reached for Sunnie's hand and escorted her to the front door. Theo opened the door to greet them, "Mr. & Mrs. Lawson, welcome home. For a moment, you two reminded me of Mr. & Mrs. Willow. So how was Italy?"

"Thanks for the compliment. Italy was heavenly," Sunnie swooned.

"Excuse me, Theo. I must carry this beautiful bride over the threshold," Cole told him as he reached to sweep Sunnie up into his arms. Sunnie giggled.

"But of course, sir," Theo said, with a wide, approving smile, as he stepped aside for the couple to enter their new home.

Sunnie looked up at her handsome husband and kissed him. She was married to the love of her life and now owned a successful horse farm.

In her wildest imaginations, Sunnie could have never anticipated that her life could be so wonderful. Her life was truly now *A Kentucky Dream* come true.

For more information on Author Susie Tillman
or to contact her, go to:

www.bearheadpublishing.com

CPSIA information can be obtained at www.ICGtesting.com
Printed in the USA
LVOW060742081111

254016LV00001B/6/P